WINDOWS ON THE WORLD

Happy reading!
May 2011
Andrea

windows
on the
world

ANDREA WHITE

namelos
South Hampton, New Hampshire

First edition

Library of Congress Cataloging-in-Publication Data

White, Andrea
Windows on the world / Andrea White.—1st ed.
p. cm.

Summary: In 2083, orphan Shama Katooee, who
has just stolen an expensive pet bird, is mysteriously
selected to attend the elite Chronos Academy to be
trained in the practice of TimeWatch, although she
has no idea how or why she has been given this honor.

ISBN 978-1-60898-105-2 (hardcover : alk. paper)
ISBN 978-1-60898-106-9 (pbk. : alk. paper)
ISBN 978-1-60898-107-6 (ebk.)

[1. Time travel—Fiction. 2. Birds—Fiction. 3.
Orphans—Fiction. 4. Schools—Fiction.
5. Science fiction.] I. Title.

PZ7.W58177Wj 2011
[Fic]—dc22
2011003678

namelos
www.namelos.com

Dedicated to the great people of New York City

"The past is never dead. It's not even past."
—*William Faulkner*

"Now he has departed from this strange world
a little ahead of me. That means nothing.
People like us, who believe in physics, know
that the distinction between past, present and future
is only a stubbornly persistent illusion."
—*Albert Einstein*

PROLOGUE

Chronos Academy
UPCITY D.C.
2083
0100 HOURS

Lieutenant Bazel typed the last string of temporal and spatial coordinates into the QuanTime—095:30:^978:&5 20:)9/11@10:24:2001—and settled onto his stool to watch.

While Bazel waited for the machine to focus, he tapped his fingers impatiently against the counter. An anonymous tip was unusual but not unheard of. Probably a lower-level employee had spotted something, and his boss had refused to give him the time needed to investi gate. That would make sense.

Bazel had programmed the lens to train outward from the doorway of a coffee shop called Starbucks, and now he found himself wishing for an old-fashioned espresso. From his studies at the Academy, he knew that the early twenty-first-century coffee shops didn't goop up their products with vitamins, like the vitacoffee shops of 2083.

Yawning, Bazel glanced at his communicator. It was late, 0122. He was a highly experienced operative of Chronos, the elite unit guarding time, and as such, he fully expected this tip to be another false alarm. Still, when he heard a click, he leaned in closer to the screen.

In the midst of the gray background, he noticed a telltale shimmer of air, the mark of the convergence of time zones, and then the picture emerged.

In the background, the one tower still standing was blurry. He could barely make it out in a fog of flames and smoke. But closer to the lens, a figure covered in dust raced by, surprising for her youth. By the length of the girl's skirt, which had the look of a uniform, and the fluid way she moved, Bazel guessed she couldn't be older than twelve or thirteen. The girl didn't look back, just ran as fast as she could, and Bazel felt happy that she seemed poised to escape the destruction.

Long ago, Bazel had wanted to run away like that, from his own personal nightmare, but he had been trapped in an apartment. It was this memory, or perhaps the girl's youth, that kept his gaze fixed on her.

He started when a piercing squeal sounded.

The QuanTime's alarm, an alert icon, flashed on the screen, and a bright red cursor pointed at an object carried by the girl, her dusty purse.

"Paaa," a sound of disgust escaped Bazel's lips. This had to be a QuanTime malfunction, the purse looked ordinary in the extreme.

Anticipating the collapse to the second, Bazel retracted the zoom for a wider view just in time to see the sides of the remaining tower suck in as if someone had tightened its belt. The metal giant swayed.

Although Bazel had programmed the QuanTime to watch the historical cataclysm, he was not prepared for the ferocity of the volcanic cloud that boiled down the valley between the buildings. Ash and pulverized concrete completely obscured the view. As the rushing wind died, he heard screams.

Bazel scooted to the edge of his stool.

The cursor pointed at something small and hard to identify in the slowly settling clouds of dust. He zoomed in on the object just as it flew toward the ground. It was the girl's purse, dust-covered, but vaguely pink. He was certain that she had been out of range of the collapse. The girl must have dropped it when she heard the blast.

Bazel had started to turn away when the purse landed on the sidewalk. Staring into its bright pink interior, he made out the bold, uneven scrawl of youth—MAYE JONES, St. Pius School—on an ID tag.

Its contents spilled: a tube of lipstick, some coins and bills, and a pencil. The cursor slid from the purse, tracking a clump of dust that detached from its side.

Not dust, a feather.

Bazel watched the cursor stay fixed on the feather as it spun and floated toward the ground. Puzzled, he scanned the feather into the analytics program.

"Year of object origination?" he asked the QuanTime.

"2083."

"Repeat! Year of origination?"

"2083."

Bazel kept his gaze trained on the feather.

"Biological classification?"

"Plumage from BriZance bird, Model no. 1. Activation Date..."

Bazel's hand trembled as he transferred the data on the feather into a confidential file, one that only he could access.

A feather from 2083 had shown up in 2001! This could be the break he had been waiting for; an opportunity to prove his theories at last.

No longer tired, he typed a request into the analytics program: *Locate all DNA matches*. It was imperative that he track down that BriZance bird and the girl, Maye Jones, fast.

Shama Katooee gazed at the egg sitting in the back of the shop. It was smaller than a puffer ball, about the size of a dodo's eye, with bands of bright purple, green, orange and pink striping its sides. She studied the sign above the cage.

BriZance bird: the ultimate pet

Shama ducked behind the counter and pressed her finger against the glass walls of the cage. As she traced the egg's oval shape, she felt a buzz all over her body but mainly in her head. She had felt the buzz a lot lately at different times and places. But in this case, she figured she must have touched an ionic current, an invisible fence to protect the bird. No matter the reason—everything seemed clearer than usual, and suddenly she had to know: Where did this beautiful egg come from?

She turned to the man behind the counter, the owner of Fankenstein 24-Hour Pet Emporium. Despite his fresh skin, the telltale wrinkles on his lips gave away his advanced age.

Shama looked up again at the sign and asked, "What's 'ultimate' mean?"

Fank glared at her ragged T-shirt and matted hair.

"What are you doing back here?" he said sharply. "Customers aren't allowed behind the counter."

"What is *that?*" Shama insisted, pointing to the egg.

"Can't you read?"

"I can read. I watch teleschool."

"Ahh, yes." The man nodded his head, as if that answered his question.

Then he looked at the BriZance. His wrinkled lips puckered with pride. "*That* is a new invention, the most expensive pet I stock. When that egg hatches, the bird bonds with its owner's DNA for life and will only go to him. Now, scoot to the front of the store where I can watch you."

"What's Deenay?"

The man rolled his eyes, the whites dyed red. "You teleschool kids don't know much. DNA is DNA. Now get out from behind here."

The door's microchip burst into a greeting—somebody was entering the shop. Fank sucked in his breath.

"Oh no! Easypawn!" he whispered, but Shama heard him.

Shama remembered Easypawn from a year or two ago. The son of a pawn shop owner in the neighborhood, Easypawn was addicted to Flay, a designer drug that supercharged your memories but destroyed your brain. Shama had seen him toss someone's pet dodo to a pack of stray wolfdogs. He and his friend Nylon bet on how long it would take the wolfdogs to rip the bird to pieces. Easypawn had won: 108 seconds. She hadn't seen him again—until now.

Nylon was right behind him. Crouching at the end of the counter, Shama watched and listened as the two men entered the store.

"Fank, you owe us. Time's up."

Nylon was doing the talking. He was scary, maybe even scarier than Easypawn. Sleep encrusted his eyes. His greenish hair was shaggy and drool foamed out of the side of his mouth. But worst of all, one side of his face was rounder than the other; a cheek implant had collapsed.

"I'll have it for you tomorrow," Fank said. His high voice trembled.

"No more excuses," Nylon said.

A harsh click sounded, and Shama saw a blue ray sizzle across the counter.

Fank yelled, "No! Don't! Please! I'm not lying to you. I swear it."

The pain beam, set to kill, lit up the BriZance's cage, melting a hole shaped like a jagged diamond in the glass wall.

As Shama watched, the striped egg jiggled. The beam must have unsettled it.

Not stopping to think, Shama reached up and thrust her hand through the hole. She scooped up the tiny egg. The egg was hot, and the buzzing feeling that had bothered her earlier returned.

"Hey, Nylon," Easypawn yelled. "Someone's here."

Shama looked in the direction of his voice.

At the far end of the counter, Easypawn stood grinning at her. His blue dust goggles were pushed back on his forehead to reveal the mounded curves of his expensive cheekbones.

"Who is it?" Nylon demanded. He kept his weapon aimed at Fank.

"A kid. That slave for the old witch Poppers," Easypawn said.

"Deal with her," Nylon said. "I'll take care of Fank."

Shama's mouth felt dry, and she swallowed to conjure up some spit.

Fank pleaded, "Please! We can work things out." He held up his hands.

In one motion, Shama slipped the egg in her pocket and crashed through a display. Boxes and cans tumbled to the floor. As she raced down the aisle to the back door, the Rabirs—*Our finest rat-bird blend!*—chirp-squealed and threw themselves against their cages.

"She's getting away!" Nylon shouted.

Before the door slammed shut, Shama heard Easypawn say, "That alley's blind." His voice sounded hauntingly calm. "I'll get her."

He's right, Shama thought, facing the back of the old bombed-out World Council Building. The ruined remains of its high walls blocked the alley's exit. She looked around and confirmed that she had no choice but to try to climb the blackened building to the roof. Starting up, splinters pierced her skin. They hurt, but not enough to stop her from climbing.

She was almost to the top when she heard Easypawn laugh, and despite the heat, she felt a chill.

"You gonna solve my problem for me—have yourself a nice accident," he said. "Those beams won't take your weight."

As Shama pulled herself to the top, she felt her heart pounding against her chest. The black skeleton of the charred building spread out before her, and she knew this route was her only choice. But all of the beams were scorched black, and most were broken and dangling. Only a few thin beams spanned the breach between the walls.

Shama put her foot on the nearest unbroken beam to test her weight. When it held, she began scooting across. *Speed won't help if Easypawn has a weapon*, she thought, but she didn't dare turn to check. That's when she had an idea.

The night with the dodo. Easypawn likes to bet.

"I bet you—" Shama liked the taunting rhythm of her voice. So unlike the fluttery feeling in her stomach. "I can make it across."

For a moment, no response and then she heard his laugh. It sounded hard and mean. "You're on," Easypawn said.

And she had the spooky feeling that he had just lowered his pain beam.

"I bet you'll end up in the pit," Easypawn called out.

The pit—the building's floor had been ripped up opening a three-story basement, known on Flade Street as the pit. On her trips there looking for scraps to sell, Shama had explored safes that used to hold credit coins but were long since looted and empty. She'd seen packs of Armaracs, disgusting raccoon/armadillo blends, nesting in the dark corners, alongside mounds of garbage and stagnant pools of human and animal waste.

The beam she balanced on creaked and sagged, as if it were about to break.

Easypawn laughed again. "Think of it as a swimming pool. Except that the water is black."

Shama's heart sank, but then she remembered the egg in her pocket and knew she had to make it. Not only for herself, but for the egg, too.

The next beam over looked nearly as weak, but she gave a little jump, and when she landed, she could feel through the soles of her sandals that the scorched material was xiathium, the virtually indestructible core support of the structure.

A piece of good luck.

Shama crouched as low as she could. She kept moving forward until she had almost reached the center of the building.

"You're at the weakest part. Now, into the pit for you!" Easypawn shouted.

Easypawn couldn't know this, but Shama's biggest problem wasn't the beam's strength but its width. Her feet almost draped over its sides. She could barely tell where the black beam ended and the dark air began, and she didn't want to look down.

If she spotted the dark belly of the burnt-out building, she might lose her nerve. "I can do this," Shama told herself as she fixed her gaze on the shop on the other side of the street, Patriotic Holostatues and Souvenirs.

"You're Armarac meat," Easypawn shouted.

She figured just twenty or so more steps. To give herself courage for the final push, she called out, breathing hard, "You lose. I'm going to make it."

Easypawn shouted, his tone one of disgust. "I should have shot you! But it don't matter. We know where you live."

Her fingers clutched the rough edge of the building—

safe! She scrambled down the frame until she got close enough to the street to jump. Her feet thumped the sidewalk, and without a backward glance, she raced down Flade Street away from Fank's pet store. Away from Easypawn and Nylon.

But Easypawn was right; they knew where she lived.

Shama ducked underneath a metallic shade-tree. In the shadows near the trunk, she squatted, satisfied that no one could see her. She slipped her hand in her pocket and carefully removed the egg. It still felt almost hot, and it wiggled in her palm.

There were cracks in it, and a tiny piece had fallen out. As Shama watched, the egg wiggled again, and another piece of shell broke off. Then a purple head with a red beak and green topknot poked out. The bird's orange eyes peered intensely at Shama.

"Sweet bird," she said.

As if to show off, the bird ruffled its wings. Color after color rippled and glowed.

Shama glanced up through the twisted dark branches of the metallic tree at the UpCity, where all the rich people lived. From Earth, it looked like a brilliant white star, surrounded by ads blazing with red, green, purple and blue. Peoplecolor: *Be the color you want to be.* Fastgrow: *Overnight you will trip on your hair.* 3-D CopyTrav: *The fastest way to travel.* Dream Hat: *A camera for your dreams.* She studied the bird again. Its sparkling feathers captured every single hue in the night sky, and like the UpCity ads, they shone as if lit from inside.

Unable to believe her good luck, Shama nuzzled the bird's green topknot. "My own fuzzy piece of sky."

With the bird cupped in her hand, Shama ducked out from under the tree and ran down Flade Street to Poppers' Radiant Laundry.

"You won't like Poppers, the lady I live with. So I'm not going to introduce you," Shama told the bird. "Best if you stay quiet."

As she walked up to the front door, an embedded microchip sang out in Poppers' shrill voice, *"Don't be a slob! Get Clean NOW."* She pressed her finger to an identification pad. The door slid open and she stepped inside. Usually the supersonic cleaning machines whirred louder than a lifter, but not this late. The shop was closed.

Poppers sat in her wheelchair behind a protective iron cage. Lots of storekeepers used them. With few police patrolling, it was their security system. Poppers had let Shama stay when her mother died. She bragged to everyone, "I take care of this poor orphan. I don't know what would happen to her if it weren't for me." But she didn't tell them about the rent she charged Shama or the countless errands she made her run.

Through the bars of the cage, Shama could see Poppers' most prominent feature, her mouth, covered in bright red permanent lip-dye.

Poppers popped a zero-calorie brownie into her cavernous mouth the second she noticed Shama.

"I'll take my gum now, Shama."

She meant the large order of estatico gum that she had

ordered Shama to pick up that night at 3 a.m. Some of the gum Poppers would lock up in her private stock and the rest Shama would hawk on the streets, with the profit going to Poppers.

"Well you see—" Shama began.

"No!" Poppers screamed. The yellow curls on her head shook with anger.

The soft feel of the bird's feathers in Shama's hand gave her something to look forward to. After Poppers finished yelling, she could play with the bird. This thought helped her to answer calmly, "The shop was closed."

Poppers' too-red lips melted into a wide frown. "Because *you* were late!"

Not true. Shama had arrived early. The mistake she made was stepping into Fank's for just a minute…

Poppers glared at Shama through the bars of the personal security cage. "No chips for you tonight."

"Poppers," Shama protested. "It was a long walk; I'm hungry."

"Everyone wants something from me," Poppers grumbled. "This customer needs his laundry done in five minutes. That one demands a special delivery. Another one has a dinner party tonight and wants a stain radiated from her tablecloth…"

"I'm not asking you for a favor. You owe me."

"Then you should have brought the gum," Poppers said. "I'm almost out." She smacked her lips as if to emphasize her empty mouth.

Shama wanted to rush over to the cage and rattle its bars. To shout at her: *You Flay zombie! You radioactive old maid! You pile of toxic ash-dung! You rabid Armarac!* But she knew it was no use, and she turned to go when she felt the bird pop out of her hand. Shama's heart caught as she watched it flying for the first time. With each beat of its wings, the bird's color changed from glowing purple to red to green to blue. It was the one beautiful thing in the otherwise gray store.

"Where did you get that?" Poppers asked.

After circling the space between them, the bird aimed for Poppers.

Don't, Shama thought. "These two Flayhead drug dealers..." As she approached Poppers' cage, she talked fast. "...were beating up this old man." But the bird flew too high overhead for her to catch it. "When I rescued him— "

"Spare me the lies," Poppers interrupted.

While Shama watched, the tiny bird dived between the bars straight at Poppers' face.

Poppers squealed and slapped the air. "Get that beast away from me." She grabbed at the bird, but it dodged her gnarled hand. Then the creature dipped and gently brushed by the old lady's cheek.

"See. The bird just wanted to give you a little kiss."

"I'll show it what a kiss is," said Poppers, grabbing again and getting nothing but air.

Come back, bird! Before she hurts you. The bird flew through the bars and landed on Shama's shoulder.

"You're useless, Shama Katooee," Poppers said. "Take that bird and get out of my sight."

Her stomach grumbling, Shama had no choice but to turn toward the washers that lined the wall. A few cleaned old-fashioned cloth, but most were radiators, used for cleaning Breathe fabric. *So much like skin, it breathes.* The secret entrance to the alcove Shama lived in was a washer that had been broken for five years. It was the one in the corner with a yellow UNDER REPAIR sign hanging above. Poppers had added a hand-written note: *Don't complain. Just take your business elsewhere.*

When Poppers got really angry with her, she threatened, "I'm going to fix that machine. And you'll have to live on the streets."

As Shama crawled through the stomach of the washer, a sharp tap on her back startled her. Then she realized that it was just the bird. Its claws hooked through her shirt.

I'm happy to be your horse, little bird.

As she felt its wings flutter in response, Shama pushed open the loose panel at the back of the washer and jumped onto a hard floor. Although her food cabinet was empty, the strong smells of the curry and pepper lingered in her room. Majong Pyler, owner of the Mystery Meat Restaurant next door, used lots of spices to flavor his entrees.

If smells were meals, I wouldn't always be hungry.

The bird flew away from her, circled the chair where her mother used to sit, and rested on the naked laser light-ball hanging from the ceiling.

Gazing at the room—nothing more than an unfinished access space for servicing the radiators—Shama said, "I'm sorry. Not a very nice home for an expensive bird."

The bird, its eyes orange dots in the dusky light, peered down at her.

"The most expensive pet I got," Fank had said.

And now she's mine. And I've got to protect her.

She hurried over to the rusty door. She never used it. It led to the alley between Poppers' Radiant Laundry and Mystery Meat Restaurant. Since she always entered and left through Poppers' front door, everyone assumed she lived inside the shop with Poppers.

But this was no protection. If Easypawn came looking for her, she knew Poppers would immediately point a fat, quivering finger in the direction of her broken washing machine.

The safest plan might be to unlock the door. That way, if she heard noises from Poppers', she could escape into the alley. She was considering whether to speak the key-words that sprang the magnetic lock when a deep male voice on the other side of the door announced: "Hologram."

Of course, it could be Nylon or Easypawn trying to trick her to open the door, but she didn't think so. Flayheads usually just knocked down doors.

She had skipped teleschool last week, but Officer Dare, the teleschool truant officer, wouldn't be bothering her at her private door. He'd go tattle to Poppers during the day— like he always did.

Shama pressed her ear to the door. It was warm even though the sun wouldn't be up for another couple of hours.

"Hologram for Shama Katooee," the voice said.

No one had ever sent Shama a holomessage before. She puckered her lips to make her voice high and began, "*Bar-la-for-jee.*" She had been six years old when her mother had helped her record her nonsensical voice key. It had been so long since she opened the lock, she was afraid that the voice chip would fail to recognize her older, deeper voice. But the magnets clicked, and the door swung open.

A holoman hovered on the sidewalk—a full-size one. Although holograms appear solid, they are only air—really nothing at all. This one looked almost human, except he glowed as if he had swallowed a laser light-ball. He was taller than most people in real life, even those in the rich neighborhoods where they got plenty to eat, but he stood stooped as if he was set to enter her door. The dark hair that topped his head matched his eyes, but not his gray eyebrows. His skin was pocked as if he had been too poor to afford the superpox vaccine as a child. He wore a funny tan cap with three stars, one brighter than the other.

Suddenly Shama heard, *Don't be a slob! Get clean NOW!* Somebody had activated the door to Radiant Laundry.

"Hologram for Shama Katooee," the holoman repeated.

"Are you sure you don't want the laundry?" Shama said, even though she knew that holomessengers lacked the ability to interact. They were programmed to deliver messages, not communicate.

Next door, Poppers' personal cage whirred.

Worry flared in the back of Shama's brain. It wasn't like Poppers to admit a customer after hours. Could someone have broken in?

Better to be ready in case she needed to escape. "Bird," Shama called. When she glanced over her shoulder, she saw the bird sail down from the lightbulb and land on her arm. She reached up and patted the bird. "Stick with me."

Before she left, the holoman standing between her and

the alley posed a mystery she wanted to solve. The holoman had said her name, had said, "Shama Katooee."

Shama reached into her pocket for her identity wand, a blue stick the length of her hand. The World Council required everyone to carry this wand that held medical history, fingerprints and Shama didn't know what else, at all times. As she had seen people on the imagetube do, Shama waved the wand in front of the holoman's face so it could authenticate her identity.

Its dark eyes scanned the wand before he said, "I am Lieutenant Bazel. I am pleased to inform you that you have been awarded a full scholarship to the Chronos Academy, room, board and clothing included. You are to come with me immediately. Arrangements for transport from the Lifter Station have been made."

"What? You must be kidding. What's the Chronos Academy?" Shama protested. Then to herself, she muttered, "Stop asking questions. You know he can't answer."

From the other room, she heard a voice. "Just shut up, old lady. Where's the kid?"

Easypawn.

The holoman was pulsing light. Shama wondered how long it would stand there.

Whirr. Whirr. Poppers was heading toward the broken machine.

As Shama looked at the room where she had lived all thirteen years of her life, she remembered the safe she kept underneath her cot. It contained a few certificates of achievement from elementary teleschool; a pair of house shoes that her mother had loved; her communicator, worthless because she couldn't pay the fees; and a locket with a photo of her mother. She was about to race for the cot to retrieve the locket when she realized that she no longer felt the prick of claws on her shoulder. Her heart rose in her throat as she called out, "Bird!"

She heard a rustling noise.

The brightly colored bird hopped backward out of a crumpled bag of Mish Mash chips on the floor.

"Bad bird," Shama said. A loud thump on the other side of the wall spooked her. "Come on. We need to leave."

When the bird landed on her shoulder, Shama hurried out into the trash-filled alley, without a backward glance.

NEW YORK CITY
SEPTEMBER 11, 2001
5:58 A.M.

The red and yellow devil roared as it lunged at her. Maye Jones tried to scream but she couldn't breathe. She tried to run but she couldn't seem to move. Her face, her body and her clothes melted inside the monster's deep black mouth. With a burst of effort, her hand smacked something hard. Pain lanced her, and her eyes flashed open.

Maye saw the white bedpost, which her knuckles had hit. She recognized the familiar pinks and blues of the checked coverlet. Inside and out, everything matched. This was her bed; she was wearing her blue cotton pajamas.

Her pajama top was wringing wet.

She turned and gazed in the direction of the roar.

No red and yellow devil. Just a simple black object with a silver rim, a digital clock radio. It read:

5:59 A.M.
SEPTEMBER 11

Shama admired the gleaming lifter, a Moonbeam 293. To handle its weight and long boxy shape, three rows of wind vents angled its body. As she stepped inside, the holoman said, "No pets allowed. Hide the bird. Stay as inconspicuous as possible."

When she glanced back, the spot where the holoman had been standing was empty, just a patch of sidewalk. "Hide the bird" was clear. But what did the holoman mean by "Stay as inconspicuous as possible?"

Just then, the lifter's wind vents engaged for take-off. Shama scooped the bird off her shoulder and thrust it into the baggy pocket of her old utility shorts. "This is your new home," she whispered to the creature. "You're so tiny, you have plenty of room. I don't want to hear any complaining." When the bird remained completely still, she wondered if it were pouting. "We all have stuff we don't like to do," she told it as she stepped inside the lifter. Like this Academy.

As she sat down on the seat, Shama looked around for clues. The compartment was small but rich looking, the HOT/COOL cushions were soft, and the bot driver didn't even have the tiniest bit of rust behind his rounded ears. Then she peered out the window, searching the storefronts for the stooped holoman who had accompanied her. *Implant Salon. Dream Hat Store. Vita-coffee shop. Food Equipment— Sale on FoodNOWs.* She could see no sign of him.

As the black and yellow lifter taxi rose from earth, Shama kept her eyes fixed on the green tin roof of her home. She had assumed that Chronos Academy was just across town, so she was surprised when the taxi-lifter didn't level out at forty meters but kept rising toward the red, blue and green gaseous highways in the sky.

She wasn't traveling across town; she was headed to the UpCity!

Shama stuck her hand in her pocket and stroked her bird's head. *We're moving up in the worlds!*

The bird nuzzled her finger as if in agreement.

As the lifter's wind vents purred, Shama found herself drifting off to sleep.

The wheels engaged, jolting the lifter, and Shama's eyes shot open. By the look of her surroundings, she guessed that the lifter had landed in some kind of terminal, enclosed in gray walls.

The bot driver twisted his head toward her. His features were all Pleasant Design: wide eyes, snub nose and designer freckles shaped like stars. "Your exit. UpCity D.C.," he announced.

As Shama stood, the door slid open. It was chilly outside. Wondering if her bird was cold, too, she stuck her hand in her pocket, but it was empty. Scanning the ceiling, she found that one of the windows was cracked, and she panicked. But then she spotted the bird perched on a nearby ledge, cleaning its wings. Looking at the brightly colored bird, Shama experienced that mysterious buzz again, and suddenly she knew that this bird understood her whether she talked out loud or not.

Bird! Come.

When Shama held out her hand, the bird left its perch and flew to her, landing on her extended finger.

Stay right here. She set it on her shoulder.

As she exited the lifter and stepped out onto the platform, a blast of cold air swirled through the building.

The place was enormous and the walls were clean without graffiti. No other vehicles were in sight.

Shama looked up toward the open roof, and for the first time in her life saw an early morning sky, empty without an UpCity looming above her. This wasn't the same sky that people on earth saw. With an UpCity blocking their view, they barely saw the sky at all. This world and its blue sky were clear, clean and beautiful.

She felt the bird's wings beat in her pocket and she recognized the same feeling in herself: she was happy.

Noises drew Shama's attention back to the ground, where a group of five or six kids waited on a narrow strip of sidewalk within the terminal, not far from her. A gated wall cut through the whole building. The wall, its flat xiathium scales vertically layered like an Armarac's, was twice as tall as Shama.

Shama guessed that the wall hid a transport station.

Just then, the lifter took off, and the dust thickened into a dark storm, biting and stinging her face. She squeezed her eyes shut.

"Hide the bird," the holoman had said.

While the storm still raged, Shama scooped the bird from her shoulder and slipped the fuzz ball into her pocket.

In protest, the bird threw itself against the fabric.

Stop it! The truth was that Shama knew exactly how the bird felt. If she were hidden away in someone's pocket, she'd have a tantrum, too.

I'll take you out as soon as I can.

When the bird finally calmed into quivering fluff, Shama approached the group.

A girl with green eyes and a coat with a flashing sign that said Ace Catholic stood apart from the other four in front of the gate. She must come from another UpCity, Shama decided. She looked too clean and neat for a LowCity.

"Are you going to the Academy?" Shama said as she approached her.

"Yes," the girl said.

"Exactly what kind of school is it?" Shama asked.

The girl's eyes, the color of pickle chips, darted back and forth nervously, as if to make sure no one was listening before she answered.

"It's the best school there is," she said, as if she'd been trained to give that answer.

"Do you really want to go?" Shama asked.

"It's a big honor," the girl said, eyes darting away again. "Excuse me," she said, turning back to the gate. "I don't want to miss anything."

Shama followed her gaze and noticed the gate's lock for the first time. It was shaped like a large X, and covered in shiny tan and gold paint. The metal was solid and smooth, no cracks or fissures at all.

Suddenly, a song blasted: the familiar lyrics of the Giant Burn hit.

As Shama stuck her hand in her pocket to calm the bird down, she saw that one of the boys was carrying a Malad, a new type of portable musicblender. *Mix street sounds. Your own. And band voices. To create new hits.* It was a red plasmonic dot the size of an old-fashioned watch-face, with record and play buttons.

The boy had a tight muscular body, and his hair was cut so short that she could see a mole on the crown of his head. It looked like a piece of dark corn.

He held up a finger and sang in a falsetto voice, "... though my grass is gone."

The bird was still thrashing around in Shama's pocket.

You can't come out now. Go to sleep.

The bird's body tightened.

I mean it. She felt the bird settle into a ball.

Good bird.

A girl with deep dimples wandered over and tapped the boy on the shoulder. He muted the musicblender and ionized it to his wrist.

As Shama listened to them, she guessed they were going to the Academy, too.

"This place sure is a howl."

"I can't believe we can't call our friends or anything."

"Or even have a communicator."

"That burns."

"My dad says if I can make it here, I'm set for life, though."

"That's what the dean at my prep school told me."

"Wow!" said someone behind Shama.

When she turned around, she saw that the girl with green eyes was staring at the lock.

Something was clicking, and the X had started to flatten into a bar. The gate was sliding open.

From the sidewalk, the wall seemed to enclose an empty lot. But when she passed through the gate, Shama was astonished to find herself facing a tall structure that should have been visible from the other side. Something weird was going on.

A building had appeared out of nowhere. It rose several hundred meters above the terminal floor and looked like a series of spoked wheels, stacked on each other. The base widened above the fence, then narrowed again to a tower that climbed to a sharp peak topped by a sphere. Outside stairwells and curved walks linked each level, and the whole thing resembled a castle made of machine parts.

The front door of the building slid aside, and the boy with the musicblender said, "Icy!"

"What is it?" the girl said. "How...?" she sputtered.

"Invisible weaponry. This building must be surrounded by a laser curtain camouflaged to look like air," the boy answered.

Another voice piped up, "Those doors are some kind of metamaterial!"

As they moved inside, Shama found herself in a strange low-ceilinged tunnel. She had never seen snow, but now she imagined that the walls, ceiling and floor of the tunnel were made out of frozen panels of the stuff. The walls radiated colors, pale shades of pink, green, blue—depending on the angle of the light—and sparkled like a trillion tiny diamonds.

Without warning, beams of light burst from every angle of the hallway. Shama had seen these SNOOP machines in holomovies. Transport stations and fancy places used them to ferret out spies and rebels, but she had never been screened before. As the beams criss-crossed her, she squirmed.

"Stand still!"

The command came from nowhere.

Shama stood tense and stiff as she imagined the light beams soaking up the number of freckles on her body, the color of her moles, the length of her big toes, her chances of her living past one hundred, and... Shama's head hurt thinking about all the possibilities.

Since the kids around her were quiet, she guessed that the SNOOPs must be commonplace in their lives. Her bird didn't seem annoyed either. Shama could feel it calmly breathing.

The lights stopped. She blinked and, a few paces in front of her, she saw a man with furry sideburns standing behind a table looking at a dataplate. He was wearing a tan military uniform like the holoman's.

Propped on the table was a sign:

AUDIO/VIDEO RECORDING IS PROHIBITED BY
COMMAND RULE 120, 453.
ANTI-SPYING SURVEILLANCE IS OPERATIONAL AT ALL TIMES.
ALL PERSONAL ELECTRONICS PROHIBITED.

The boy who had sang the Giant Burn song stood in front of the table.

"I'm Dean Perbile," said the man.

The man's complexion was reddish around the edges—the tops of his ears, his hairline—and yellow in the middle of his face. Shama thought he had the perfect name: he looked like the parboiled potatoes she'd seen in huge vats at the Chip Factory.

"Your name?" Dean Perbile said. The part of his head visible from underneath his cap was as bare as drought-scorched earth, but he scratched one of his bushy side-burns that grew like vines.

"Peke Zorn," the boy said. "I'm from the Indian district of Old Delhi."

"Welcome," the Dean said, but his smile didn't reach his eyes. Then she noticed something really spooky. His right eye was a Wander Eye, modified to allow it to rotate around in its socket and see at wide angles.

The Dean held out his hand. "The musicblender."

The boy stuck his hand in his pocket and placed the expensive device in the Dean's outstretched palm.

Deliberately, the Dean tossed it into a box by his feet.

When Shama peered inside the box, she saw a pile of communicators, musicblenders and a bright new RACM portal. Suddenly she worried about the little bird resting trustfully in her pocket. "Hide the bird," the holoman had said.

I won't go to this school if I have to give you up!

Shama wondered why the surveillance device hadn't picked up the bird. Maybe it had something to do with what Fank said.

That's when it came to her. The perfect name for her bird.

You're Deenay!

With that the bird rose up and tried to escape her pocket.

Shama put her hand in and stroked its topknot. *Not now. Just a little bit longer.*

The bird settled down in the pocket. *Make it quick*, it seemed to say.

"Uniforms are in the changing rooms," Dean Perbile said to Peke Zorn. "Then, head to the Auditorium."

The boy nodded and started walking down the hallway. He didn't even glance at his musicblender. Dean Perbile was already talking to the next person in line. Soon it was Shama's turn.

"Name?"

"Shama Katooee."

With a frown, Dean Perbile gazed at his dataplate, scrolling down names and identification numbers. Shama felt her heart beating faster. Of course, there must have been some mistake. It wasn't only her bird that didn't belong here. She didn't belong.

Although his regular eye stayed glued to the page, when his Wander Eye fixed on her, the dark orb seemed to know everything about her. Including all her misdeeds. Selling estatico gum was illegal. Her heart was pounding when finally he mumbled, as if to himself, "Late addition."

Shama blew out the breath she'd been holding. *We're going to be O.K.*, she thought and felt a slight answering flutter.

Dean Perbile met her gaze. "You need to come see me later today. I have some questions about your records."

When she nodded, Dean Perbile waved her on.

"Follow the rest of them."

Walking down a tunnel with glass walls, a glass ceiling and a glass floor made Shama feel disoriented, and after a few steps, she reached out and touched the wall. She turned her gaze back just as the tunnel opened out into a high-ceilinged rotunda.

Clusters of glass-walled rooms stacked on top of each other. A series of staircases connected the rooms. A few seemed to stop at nothing, going nowhere, but remembering the laser curtain around the building, she sensed there were more rooms than she would ever see or enter.

The air was cool, chilly even, and it didn't smell like fried chips and Flay, curry and pepper, dirt and sweat or anything at all that she was used to on Earth. She didn't spot a speck of dust or a bit of trash. Throngs of kids dressed in tan uniforms surrounded her, and with their shiny hair and sparkling complexions, they all looked rich. Like they had never missed a meal in their lives. They looked smart, too, like they could recite encyclopedias.

Shama hesitated just for a second. *Deenay, you and I are as good as anybody.* Then she threw back her shoulders and kept walking.

NEW YORK CITY
SEPTEMBER 11, 2001
6:05 A.M.

Leaning close to the mirror, Maye looked into her own yellow eyes; everyone said they were unusual. Unusually ugly, she thought—the color of sawdust. Her skin was the hue of wet beach sand. But she had one great feature, a perfect nose.

As she reached for the toothpaste, she threw her crinkliest smile at the mirror. For Victor Bhatt. Victor had jet black hair that shone like motor oil, straight white teeth and a dimple in his chin. From the moment she first saw him, she had a crush on him.

Although Maye had started at St. Pius a full year ago, Victor had only noticed her recently. In the last few days, she had caught him staring at her. Twice. When his eyes met hers, he had smiled, and not in an ordinary way. His smile made her feel like she was a movie star. Or at the very least, someone he wanted to invite to a movie.

She fluffed up her brown hair to hide her left ear, melted in a fire when she was a baby. *So long ago that she could no longer remember*, she thought gratefully as the mirror began shimmering.

Maye leaned in for a closer look and found that it was the air, not the mirror, that vibrated, like water disturbed by a pebble. Staring long and hard into the mirror's depths, she had the strange feeling that she could see other Mayes, other rooms and other silvery dark futures. Then, as if someone had flipped a switch, the mirror and her face became normal again.

Chronos Academy
UPCITY D.C.
2083
1021 HOURS

A girl with long blonde hair and thin lips sat on a bench in the changing room.

The girl, bent over the ionic clasp of her boots, was taller than Shama. A patch of pink speckled both of her cheeks. Her skin was pearly smooth as though she had never been in the sun.

Piles of boots, T-shirts and pants—all tan—filled glass shelves, layering the walls. Suddenly Shama understood. This wasn't a store. The clothes were free.

Shama loaded her arms and wandered over to where the girl sat next to a row of lockers and across from a mirror. Breathe fabric—*Warm you up. Cool you down. Depending on the temp*—was supposed to be comfortable, but when she slipped the first brand-new T-shirt she had ever owned over her head, she immediately felt itchy. *Weird*, she thought, *that people would pay more for stiff clothes.*

After Shama had pulled on her pants, she glanced at the girl to make sure she wasn't watching her. She was busy zipping up her sleeve to be the exact right length.

Shama nestled Deenay into the deep pocket of her new long pants.

You passed through the SNOOP machine so you have as much right to be here as me.

She stuck her hand in her pocket to stroke the bird's topknot.

Deenay pecked at her finger.

"Ouch," Shama said.

"What's wrong?" the girl said. She stood in front of the mirror and shook her legs to force her pants to fall down past her ankles.

"Oh, nothing. Just talking to myself," Shama said, holding her hand against the outside of her pocket to calm the bird. *If you don't behave, we won't be able to eat.*

The bird settled down, and Shama was able to approach the girl.

"I'm Shama Katooee," she said.

The girl raised her hand in greeting. "Hi. I'm Tres…Tres Mungo."

Tres' nails were ragged and torn like some Armarac had munched on them for breakfast, and Shama realized that she was staring at them. To cover her rudeness, she asked quickly, "What kind of place is this?"

"It's top secret and real important," Tres said, proudly.

"So tell me," Shama said. She felt Deenay begin to snuggle against her hip. *That's O.K. so long as you stay inside my pocket.*

"I'm not supposed to," Tres said. She spoke slowly, emphasizing the beginnings and endings of each word to give it its own space. "General Mungo, my father, will explain at the Orientation."

This kid is rude.

"Well, I know a lieutenant here," Shama bragged. *Okay, not exactly!* But she had met his holoman. "I guess I'll just ask him."

"That's impossible," Tres said. "You can't know anyone here. You're not from the Zone."

"I do, too."

"Who?" Tres demanded.

"Lieutenant Bazel," Shama said.

"*Bazel?*" Tres seemed genuinely puzzled now. She glared at Shama. "How do *you* know *him?*"

"We're friends," Shama said. Anyone who told her "Hide that bird" was a friend. But this thought caused her to remember the holoman's other piece of advice, "Stay as inconspicuous as possible," and she decided to change the subject.

"When's breakfast?"

"You mean lunch? After Orientation," Tres said, with a puzzled look. "Are you all right?"

The way she asked, the question sounded like "Are you weird?" not like "Are you feeling ill?"

"I'm fine."

Tres frowned, turned away, and headed out of the room.

Shama was about to take Deenay out of her pocket when a group of girls strolled in, laughing and talking. Deenay's wings fluttered then dropped. A bird sigh. Shama knew the bird was as hungry as she was.

Shama turned toward the mirror and ran her fingers through her unruly hair. A top-secret Academy in an invisible building sounded impossible, but she couldn't help hoping. Maybe, just maybe, this school was the break that she needed to get away from Poppers and the grind on Flade Street.

Besides, if nothing else works out, Shama thought, *I'll make sure that you and I get something to eat.*

Shama took a good look around the auditorium.

On Flade Street, in order to watch teleschool, Shama jammed with hundreds of kids into the public idearoom. This room was huge with empty chairs. The ceiling was incredibly high, just wasted space.

Unless you're a bird.

Shama wished she could let Deenay out of her pocket.

Dean Perbile stood in the center of a stagelike platform. Behind him were two rows of high-backed white chairs that looked like soft thrones. The Dean's Wander Eye searched every corner as if he expected chaos to break out at any moment, but Shama could already tell: these kids were the most obedient group she had ever been around.

A hololaser projector hung from the ceiling, just like at teleschool. But the teleschool projector was a plain black box with dangling cybratom tubes, and this one was a small blue- and silver-tinted glass hemisphere with an array of lenses barely visible.

"Please find seats and sit down, Cadets," Dean Perbile called out to the students who were milling around and talking.

Even though Shama was in the back of the room, it sounded as though the man spoke directly into her ear. Probably he was using an Earbone speaker like the ones in Flade Street Holotheatre, she decided.

She plopped into the first open seat and recognized immediately that it was covered in Puzz: *Peachfuzz is the softest fabric known to man.* When she felt the controls built into the arms of the chair, she realized it was probably a PAD—Personal Aviation Device—like the ones she had seen in the news coverage of World Council sessions and that this chair could fly.

That explains the ceilings! Maybe we can fly around together in here sometime.

As Shama settled into the seat, she felt Deenay shift in her pocket.

But not right now.

Shama was careful to cover her lap with her arm to hide the movement in her pocket from view.

When she lifted her gaze there was a boy sitting down next to her. She didn't know any boys like him on Earth. It wasn't just that his skin looked like it had never seen the sun. Or that he was taller than any boy she knew on Flade Street. It was something about his gray eyes—they were bright and intense—and it was the way he studied her when she said, "I'm Shama Katooee. When do we get to eat?"

"I'm Kardo Felix. Probably after this class."

He wasn't cute exactly. His ears had a super thick fold. His forehead staked out too much space. And the PAD seat forced his lanky body into a hunched position. "Even though I grew up in the Zone, this is my first time at the Academy."

"The Zone?" Tres had used that term, too.

"This whole complex," Kardo said. "How about you? Where are you from?"

"Lower D.C.," Shama said.

"Really! Wow," Kardo said as if he meant it. "What prep school did you go to?"

"What's a prep school?" Shama asked.

Kardo threw back his head and laughed. Shama liked the sound.

Suddenly Tres, the girl Shama had met in the changing room, was standing in the aisle. She frowned when she spotted Shama.

"Tres, have you met…?" Kardo asked.

Tres interrupted, "Yes. We've met."

Kardo shot Tres a look.

Tres sat down next to Kardo, rested her hand lightly on Kardo's arm and began whispering into his ear. As she did, Deenay started hopping up and down in Shama's pocket.

Stop it. Please.

Deenay quieted, settling into a ball.

Thankfully, no one was paying any attention to her.

In fact, gazing at Kardo's back, Shama felt as unimportant as a bot bum, one of the rusty old robots who panhandled for their owners. She nudged Kardo. "Hey! What's it like growing up in an invisible glass house?"

Tres glared at Shama. But Kardo turned toward her and calmly answered, "We had to live here, because of our parents' jobs. For security. But we got to go to other places on vacation sometimes."

Shama surveyed the room. "This room has so many seats. There aren't that many of us. Where is everybody else?"

"Duh," Tres said. "The upperclassmen are coming next week."

Kardo chided her gently, saying, "How could Shama be expected to know that, Tres?"

"That's exactly my point," Tres said in a low voice. "Kids coming from the outside don't know anything."

"They're coming from all over the Upper World. They know things we don't," Kardo said.

"Yeah," Shama said. "Like I bet you don't know how to wake up a sleeping Flayhead."

Tres raised one eyebrow and said coolly, "You're right. I don't."

"You pinch his toe," Shama said.

Tres rolled her eyes.

Shama had forgotten all about Deenay when she felt the bird hurl her tiny body upward. She faked a cough, doubled over and with one hand thrust the bird back into her pocket.

Before the bird could peck her, she yanked her hand away and accidentally jostled the seat in front of her.

A husky girl with no chin turned around and barked, "Hey! Watch out."

Tres shook her head as if to say, *Not me.*

"Are you O.K., Shama?" Kardo asked.

Shama smiled at both of them. "As crunchy as a new bag of barbecue bubble gum chips."

A surprised look came over Tres' face, and Tres burst out laughing.

NEW YORK CITY
SEPTEMBER 11, 2001
6:09 A.M.

Maye opened the closet and saw a few clothes and lots of empty coat hangers. If she were a normal daughter, not just a kid living with foster parents, she'd have a closet packed full of clothes and shoes like the rest of the girls at St. Pius. If her mother hadn't died in that fire...

Phew! First her nightmare and now thinking about her mother. It was too much, too early in the morning. She banged the door closed and turned away.

She dressed quickly in her St. Pius uniform: blue skirt and a white blouse. As she turned to go to breakfast, she noticed her new pink purse. A splash of color on the beat-up brown bureau.

Lynn, her latest foster mother, had given her the clutch for her thirteenth birthday.

"Are you coming, Maye?" She heard her foster father's voice urging her.

Maye snatched the purse off the counter.

Today was a field trip. Field trips were different than a school day. Field trips were special.

Chronos Academy
UPCITY D.C.
2083
1045 HOURS

Shama put her hand inside her pocket and stroked Deen-ay. As long as she paid attention to the bird, it seemed to be content.

A bell rang.

In the front of the room, two rows of uniformed men and women were lining up on the stage.

Shama spotted Lieutenant Bazel in the back. She wondered if the real man would recognize her, and she tried to catch his eye, but he was busy talking to a short man standing next to him and was too far away anyway.

When Shama got a chance, she wanted to ask him why he had sent a holoman to fetch her and why he said, "Stay as inconspicuous as possible."

A man—tall, thin, with piercing blue eyes and wispy red hair—walked to the center of the stage. More stars glittered on his cap than on Lieutenant Bazel's, and unlike the lieutenant, this man's posture was erect.

Around the room, the shuffling and coughing stopped.

"I'm General Mungo, Commanding Officer of Chronos," he announced.

The General's eyes seemed faded and old. They were pale blue, the color of Shama's favorite T-shirt. The shirt used to be her mother's, and Shama had worn it so much it was almost threadbare. Shama wished she were wearing it now.

The General gestured behind him. "Here you see the Command Staff as well as a few other operatives who will be your teachers throughout this important Orientation process."

The General turned and nodded at the thirty or so men and women and in unison, they sat down in the rows of high-backed chairs. Each of them looked important, as if their faces should be stamped on the sides of credit coins.

"I want to welcome you to Chronos Academy," General Mungo said. "It is our tradition for the Commanding General to give the first lecture."

Shama leaned closer to Kardo and whispered, "Hey, a real flesh-and-blood teacher."

Kardo looked puzzled. Shama realized he didn't watch teleschool. He'd had real teachers. Probably all of these kids had. Feeling a little embarrassed, she quickly turned her attention back to the stage.

"Some of you students have parents who attended the Academy," General Mungo said. "In fact, my own daughter is in the audience."

At her father's words, Tres sat straighter and raised her chin even higher. The blush on her cheeks deepened.

"But many of you are seeing the Zone for the first time today," General Mungo said. "Regardless of your parentage, each of you has been chosen from top-ranked schools around the Upper World because of your leadership qualities and your academic excellence, especially in history and science."

What? Shama wasn't from an UpCity school and her grades in teleschool, especially in history and science, were nothing special. In fact, they were barely okay. Well, the last time she checked, she wasn't failing.

Tres glanced at Shama, her eyebrows arched. After making sure Shama felt her skepticism, Tres turned back to the stage.

These kids may not like me, but at least I have Deenay, Shama thought, as she stroked her bird. When she didn't feel any responding pressure on her finger, she realized that the bird had fallen asleep. Finally.

"This Academy represents an amazing opportunity. You will face a variety of tests this week, and those with passing scores will be invited to enroll," General Mungo said.

"What happens if you don't pass?" Shama whispered to Kardo.

"They boil you in robot oil," Kardo said.

"You two need to listen," Tres hissed.

"I want you to take a moment and imagine that you have the ability to change history for the better," General Mungo said. He paused as if thinking hard, but Shama guessed that every line was part of a memorized script for a part he had played many times. "Why don't we start on a personal level? I know you are all idealists. Wouldn't you like to help every parent in the past who lost a child in an accident?"

A girl sitting in front of them bobbed her head in agreement. Shama recognized her as the one who had been unable to take her eyes off the gate.

General Mungo pointed at the girl.

"Those of you who are new to the Zone are going to have to help me with your names," he said.

"I'm Gleer Rodriquez. And yes, Sir, I'd love to save every kid who was ever killed in an accident."

General Mungo touched a button on the communicator he wore on his wrist, and holograms of infants, toddlers, girls and boys, teenagers appeared in the aisles of the auditorium. Mostly, they stood; some appeared mid-stride. Some jumped. One young boy somersaulted over Shama's head. His eyes were wide open and his neck tilted in a wrong way, broken.

What kind of strange class is this?

Shama turned to ask Kardo and Tres, but they looked so serious and focused that this time she didn't say anything.

"And don't you think every child who lost a parent in an accident would like to bring that parent back?" General Mungo asked.

Shama winced. Eight years ago, her mother had left on an errand to buy more firesticks to mend clothes for Poppers' customers. A lifter had lost power, fallen from the sky, and crushed Anna Katooee as she crossed the street. "I'd give anything if I could stop Mama from leaving the hut on that stupid errand."

Tres leaned over and said, "Shhh!"

Without warning, holomen and holowomen, dressed in styles from all the ages, filled the empty seats in the auditorium. In the aisle across from her, a man wearing a dress made out of metal and a helmet on his head materialized. His eyes flared in shock and surprise. Next to the warrior was a grandmother type who had on a green satin ball gown. Her mouth was frozen open in terror. A swarthy man dressed in animal skins, his face wrinkled in confusion, stood in the aisle next to her.

Shama turned away from the caveman and looked around quickly. She didn't think it was possible but she didn't want to find her mother's broken body in that crowd of holopeople.

"Of course, we can't forget all the soldiers killed in wars," General Mungo said, and more holograms appeared. The crowd filled the aisles and surrounded the stage. Soldiers in uniform. Blue with white hats. Khakis. Kilts. Green with canvas belts. Camouflage. These holopeople weren't standing straight but were cockeyed, tilted, lying down, and Shama didn't like looking at them—at their eyes filled with confusion, surprise and fear.

"Now, what about if we save all those people who died of superpox and hyperpolio before the vaccines were invented?"

Holoimages projected onto holoimages; overlays of people created a holomass, a riot of belts, hands, feet, noses, legs, dresses, pants, shoes...

"As you look around this packed room," General Mungo said, "imagine the world with one hundred thousand times the number of people we have now, many of them inventors, musicians, businessmen and teachers. All of whom would have had children and grandchildren had they not died when they did."

Perched on the edge of her seat, Shama felt smushed like she was the bottom layer in a human pie. Just as she groaned, "Let me out of here," the holopeople vanished as suddenly as they had appeared, and Shama felt she could breathe again. Relieved, she sank back down into her chair.

General Mungo continued.

"Would our history be very different if we saved millions of people from the ravages of premature death?"

He pointed at the back of the auditorium.

"Cadet Uber."

Shama craned her neck to find Cadet Uber.

The girl had a curvy figure and looked brainy. Maybe it was just the way her tight ponytail made her close-together eyes bug out.

"The world would be too crowded, Sir," Cadet Uber said.

"Right," General Mungo said.

"Now, I want all of you to try to imagine a world where you could use a machine to go back in time and save lives any time you wanted." General Mungo paused. "How do you think your actions would change our world?"

Tres raised her hand. As the general looked at his daughter, Shama studied the General's blue eyes, the set of his mouth. His expression stayed hard, and Shama felt bad for Tres—just for an instant.

"Yes, Cadet Mungo."

"History would be like a mixed-up movie with no beginning, middle or end," Tres said.

"An interesting point," General Mungo said. "There would be no history as we know it, right? History would always be changing."

Kardo held up his hand, and the General nodded.

"Sir. Someone would need to decide who should be able to change history. After all, the changes would affect all of us."

"Good point, Cadet Felix. Who do you think that person should be?" General Mungo said.

Kardo frowned. "I don't know."

"Me," Shama whispered to Kardo.

Kardo gave a short laugh, but Tres frowned.

General Mungo nodded at Gleer Rodriquez. "Who do you think should control our time machine?"

"I think the Pope should decide."

"Cadet Rodriquez, do you think the Jews, Baptists, Muslims and Spiritual Environmentalists will think that fair?"

Gleer squirmed in her seat.

General Mungo pointed at Peke Zorn, the boy who had the musicblender.

Seeing him again, Shama decided he looked like a regular kid. Someone who Shama might have known on Flade Street. Peke's posture was looser than the rest of the kids, and despite the fact that he had ignored her outside the gate, his face was friendlier and more open.

Peke introduced himself, and General Mungo said, "I'm listening, Cadet Zorn."

"A panel of religious figures could decide," Peke Zorn said.

"From every religion in the world? Or just the largest religions?" General Mungo said.

Peke Zorn shrugged. "Just the largest?"

"Would this panel be elected or appointed? Would every religion get the same number of votes?"

General Mungo waited.

"Yes, Cadet Felix."

"A time machine would create lots of problems," Kardo said.

"Very good," General Mungo said. "To go back to the point I was trying to make earlier, assuming you controlled a time machine, and you decided that you couldn't let everyone use it to have access to history, whom could you let use it?" General Mungo asked. "Yes, Cadet Uber."

"Nobody," Cadet Uber called out.

The edges of the General's mouth softened, and he almost smiled.

Shama heard Tres whisper to Kardo. "Deza, showing off again."

"Cadet Uber has raised an interesting alternative," General Mungo said. "We've established that if everyone is allowed access, time will become a mess. If only a few people are allowed access, we have the problem of who gets to decide. Now Cadet Uber has proposed a third approach. What if the only group with the ability to create a time machine decided to protect history? What if this group took an oath never to change it for any purpose whatsoever, even a noble one like saving lives?"

A number of kids raised their hands to ask more questions, but General Mungo shook his head. "It's time for me to tell you why you're here."

Shama felt herself tense.

"Dr. Lassemar invented the QuanTime machine in 2043," General Mungo said. "With the aid of its chrono-transitive lens, we can observe history as it unfolds in real time."

"Time travel?" Shama didn't mean to speak out loud

but General Mungo looked straight at her. She slunk down in her seat. Then the General redirected his attention to the whole auditorium.

"Not time travel—time watch."

"Can you watch anyone? Anywhere? Any time?" Shama asked.

"Please raise your hand and wait to be recognized before you speak out," General Mungo said.

"I told you," Tres murmured.

General Mungo frowned. "The potential destructive capability of a machine that allows human beings to travel in time is so enormous that we are pursuing that technology with great caution."

Each of the General's words had "important" smeared on it like the way Shama liked to put vitaketchup on a soy burger. With onions. Pickles. And Mish Mash chips. She sighed as General Mungo said, "When we properly use the QuanTime, we witness the past, standing firmly planted in the present."

NEW YORK CITY
SEPTEMBER 11, 2001
6:15 A.M.

Dan Jawalski stirred the pot on the gas stove with his back to Maye.

Maye could smell the heavy dose of cinnamon Dan poured into the oatmeal that he was cooking for her, and the tang of the coffee he was brewing for himself. She pulled out the chair, set the pink clutch on the breakfast table and sat down.

"Good morning, sweetie." Dan turned and faced her. He was a thin man with an Adam's apple that bobbed above a red tie. White streaked his rust-colored hair, which he wore swept back from his lined face.

"Did you have that nightmare again?" Dan asked.

Had Maye cried out? As a legal assistant for a Brooklyn law firm, Maye's foster mother worked long hours. Maye hoped that she hadn't woken Lynn. She rushed to apologize, "I'm sorry."

"It's not that," Dan said. "I was just...wondering."

Wondering if you got yourself a real weirdo for a foster kid. One who needed an expensive psychiatrist. Who might wake up one day and do something violent. "I'm fine," she said. But remembering the strange sensations that she had had that morning looking into the mirror, she felt worried.

Dan smiled and shook more brown cinnamon into the pot. "I know you are, Maybe," he said.

Maybe. Her nickname.

A sixth grade teacher who misspelled Maye's name had coined it. In the beginning, Maye hated the name and corrected everyone—"My name is Maye"—but this morning, she let it go.

Chronos Academy
UPCITY D.C.
2083
1250 HOURS

An invisible hand seemed to write, "Chronos, Time's Keeper and History's Guardian," above the stage in holographic font.

"On May 17th, 2043," General Mungo said, "Dr. Hiram Lassemar demonstrated the powers of the QuanTime to then-President Alia and her cabinet.

"President Alia wasn't impressed by Dr. Lassemar's presentation. She said, 'A time-watch machine is worthless. I order you to find a way to use the QuanTime to *change* the past.'

"Dr. Lassemar felt certain that if our government—if any government—gained the ability to redesign history to suit its own ends, life as we know it would be destroyed. To forestall this dire result, Dr. Lassemar asked me to conduct a top-secret experiment, one that would make President Alia understand what you students knew instinctively. We shouldn't advance the QuanTime to a point where it could be used to meddle in human affairs. We must remain observers, not change agents."

That's when the power of a portal like this really hit Shama. A lens like a gigantic eye stretching back through all of time could focus on the awful night seven years ago when her mother set out on her errand. Shama could warn her not to leave the hut. Such a small change, not a big deal. *History wouldn't even notice*, she thought as she felt herself tremble with excitement.

"For the experiment, Dr. Lassemar selected a disaster that occurred around the turn of the century," General Mungo said. "Who can tell me where Manhattan Island was?"

Shama had never heard of the place but many cadets raised their hands.

When General Mungo called on Cadet Zorn, Peke said, "Along with many coastal cities, the rising oceans wiped out the island about thirty years ago. While most of the cities were reestablished inland, Manhattan Island was not."

"Correct," General Mungo said. "I'm sure all you history buffs are familiar with the Twin Towers disaster."

Shama sighed. She had never heard of the Twin Towers, but again, she noticed that all around her the cadets were nodding their heads.

Next to her, Kardo murmured, "9-11."

"Modern historians believe that the Twin Towers disaster triggered the split between the Upper and Lower Worlds," General Mungo said. "That's why I choose the Twin Towers as the basis for my experiment. Are you following me?"

No one spoke up.

"In the Manhattan experiment, my scientists and I envisioned a world where we stopped Al-Qaeda, a terrorist group, from hijacking two airplanes and flying them into the pair of buildings known as the Twin Towers. We created a model showing the changes in history that would occur had the Twin Towers disaster been prevented. Our model presented history as it would have been if the victims of the Manhattan disaster had been allowed to live out their full lives."

Despite her hunger, Shama felt her interest quicken. "I've heard of remakes of holomovies." *Urban Fire Warriors, Freezer Holiday, Alamo Redux,* and *Robot Love.* "But different versions of history?" she said to Kardo.

Kardo nodded. "Weird, isn't it?"

"Obviously, under the terms of our Manhattan Experiment, the lives of the victims' families were uplifted and transformed. But what do you cadets think happened to the world at large?" General Mungo asked.

Shama sensed a trick question. *Everyone else must be suspicious, too, because no one raised a hand.*

General Mungo allowed himself a brief smile as he touched his communicator. "This holoreproduction shows a phase of our experiment."

On the stage, a gray bridge spanned a slow-moving river. Old-fashioned cars without air vents or sky hooks crowded the bridge.

"In a world without the Manhattan disaster, an earthquake shook Sydney, Australia and severely impacted the Sydney Harbor Bridge," General Mungo said. "How many people do you think died?" He nodded. "Cadet Uber?"

"The same number of people killed in the Manhattan disaster."

General Mungo smiled, a gleam in his pale blue eyes. "Correct." He shrugged. "Of course, the results could have been more subtle. The cosmic law of averages could have produced several small tragedies to yield the same outcome. But according to its design, the experiment presented its results in a straightforward fashion."

"What's he talking about?" Shama said to Kardo.

"You'd understand better if you kept quiet and listened," Tres shot back.

The holobridge's pylons began to wiggle and shake.

As vans, taxis and cars plummeted off the side, some fell into the murky water below. Others turtled onto the banks and exploded.

The water towered, splashing the cadets with shards of blue air, and the pylons began to crumple. When the bridge became a wall of jagged fire, clouds of black smoke billowed out, hiding the holoprojector.

The bridge trestle bent sideways. When it collapsed, blown by a fierce wind, pieces of metal and steel spewed toward the audience.

Even though Shama knew the scene was holographic, she had to force herself not to duck as a black beam, the size of a lifter, rushed toward her.

In front of Shama, Cadet Rodriquez gasped and slapped her hands over her eyes.

The air around Shama had grown dark, as if filled with odorless smoke, and then without warning, the stage held only the General and his Command Staff again. A line of holographic script appeared above General Mungo's head.

"The mathematical formula for the Constant of Suffering," General Mungo said, pointing at the script.

"To state this simply, the amount of suffering in the world is hardwired and constant. It cannot be altered. No matter how we hard we try, we cannot reduce mankind's pain," General Mungo said.

Shama wanted to go back to that night seven years ago and warn her mother not to leave their hut. If she couldn't do that, she thought angrily, she wanted to eat. All it would take to reduce her pain was a bag of chips.

General Mungo continued. "I can demonstrate this principle graphically and diagrammatically as well."

Shama settled back into her comfortable chair and closed her eyes. For just a minute. She had managed to forget about her aching stomach when she felt a sharp nudge.

"What?"

Hot breath tickled her ear, and she heard Kardo's voice whispering. "You fell asleep."

Shama shot upright. "Is it time for lunch?"

Maye caught a glimpse out of the breakfast room window of the only tree in the Jawalskis' small yard—an oak whose crown rose higher than the roof. In a new neighborhood, with nothing else better to do, she had spent the last summer climbing its gnarly branches, talking to the blackbirds and identifying shapes in the leaves and clouds.

Maye had always liked birds. Sometimes, she even dreamed about an unusual one. The bird had a bright green topknot, and its feathers were her favorite bright colors all mixed together: red, green, blue and purple.

Interrupting her thoughts, Dan patted her shoulder as he served her the oatmeal. It was a gesture like a father would make, but he patted too hard.

"Ouch," Maye mumbled.

Dan removed his hand and gazed sadly at her.

Chronos Academy
UPCITY D.C.
2083
1335 HOURS

FoodNOW. *Any food you want at the push of a button.* Even when Shama stood on tiptoes, the machine was a head taller than her. Buttons, symbolizing the different food groups, lined its front. A gaping metallic mouth marked the place where the food was going to appear—soon, Shama hoped. After three glasses of vitajuice, she was no longer starving. But she hadn't been able to find anything for Deenay, and inside her pocket she could feel the bird's wings flutter.

Soon, we'll eat.

More for something to do than anything else, she stuck her glass under the spout on the machine's side for another refill.

While she waited, she scoped out the cafeteria. The teachers sat around several tables mounted on a foot-high platform in front. Same as in the auditorium, they were about thirty grown-ups, half of them women. Now that she got a closer view of the group, she decided that although a few looked like military operatives should—tough and lean—most were pudgy like the clientele at Mystery Meat Restaurant, famous on Flade Street for its triple portions.

General Mungo wasn't among the group. Shama only recognized two adults. She spotted Dean Perbile, and she caught a glimpse of Lieutenant Bazel talking to a short man with a tuft of hair sticking up like a flag.

The green liquid stopped spewing from FoodNOW's spout; only a few drops trickled into the glass.

As Shama sipped the drink, she turned over her new circumstances in her mind, wondering if a machine really could let her go back and see her mother when she was alive. The ache that she felt then had nothing to do with hunger.

Shama returned to her place in line, behind the smart-looking girl who'd answered all the questions in the auditorium, Cadet Deza Uber.

Deza, her ponytail tighter and neater than any Shama had ever seen, pressed her thumb against the nutrient profile button.

"Ready for your selection," the machine said in the voice of a concerned doctor.

The bird stirred inside her pocket and started to peck her lightly on her hip.

Just a few minutes now. I'll get you some food.

She could sense the feathery puff-ball's excitement. It more than matched her own.

Deza pushed the button for soy tacos.

"Wait just a few minutes, while we supplement your meal with vitamins and minerals to optimize your caloric intake," the machine said.

"Maybe you can explain something to me," Shama said to Deza to make conversation. "How are we able to watch the past as if it were some kind of holomovie that's playing all the time?"

Behind them, Peke Zorn spoke up. "You've picked the right person to ask, but do you have about three hours for the answer?"

Deza smiled. "Give me a break, Peke." She turned to Shama. "Peke is exaggerating. Of course, I don't understand time theory yet, but I like science, especially physics, and I've studied the theories of gravity and spacetime."

Shama said, "I thought the past was over."

Deza trained her bug eyes on Shama. "Everything seems to be ordered by time, yet it all happens now. That is the paradox of advanced physics…"

Shama was about to say, "Save the details. I only care how it works," when she heard a whirring sound as Deza's tray with its beautiful food slid into the mouth of the machine.

Three tacos sat there, crammed with soy meat and crowned with green and purple sauce. As Shama breathed in the greasy, beefy smell, she was sorry she had asked Deza a question. Now that it was her turn, Shama had even less interest in physics. Besides that, Shama felt the bird try to claw its way to the top of her pocket.

Deenay, no!

As she pressed her arm against her side to box Deenay in, Shama stepped up to the FoodNOW, and pushed the button for plain soy tacos, not a designer version tailored to suit her own body. She didn't want to wait for the supplements.

She was searching for the button for *regular* chocolate cake—none of the fake stuff for her—when she realized that

Deza was still talking: "The vertical dimension of the past is accessible through the portal of the present moment." While Shama listened with one ear to Deza's explanation, sprinkled with phrases like "Quantum mechanics," "string theory" and "closed time curves," she punched the button for chocolate cake—once, twice. She crossed her fingers, hoping that the machine allowed double portions.

In a concerned voice, FoodNOW suggested, "Zero calorie cake is the healthier choice."

For an answer, Shama pushed the button a third time.

As she waited for her tray to appear, the smell of Deza's food tortured her. She kept her face turned toward FoodNOW while Deza droned on about wormholes.

"Remember anti-cancer salt will keep the doctor away," FoodNOW reminded Shama as her tacos and only one slice of chocolate cake appeared in the mouth of the machine.

Eagerly, Shama snatched the tray, and it was Peke's turn.

"So now you see why somebody said, 'Time keeps us from understanding that everything happens at once.'" Deza paused. "I hope that makes sense?'"

When Shama didn't answer, Deza's face fell. "Sorry for the quick explanation," Deza said.

Quick? "Yeah, and thanks," Shama said.

"Any time." Deza gave her a smile and walked away.

Shama broke off a piece of taco shell and dropped it into her pocket.

This should keep you for a while.

Deenay began attacking the shell.

Shama stood there with her tray, searching for a seat.

She scanned the faces in the Mess Hall, recognizing some cadets from the lecture. Gleer Rodriquez, the girl who wanted to save everybody, clutched her tray and surveyed the crowd. She acted as if she expected somebody to invite her to join a group. Then Shama saw Kardo. His thin back faced her. She was about to head toward him when she spotted Tres, sitting beside him, a scowl on her face.

Shama walked over to Deza's table and plopped down a few seats away from her.

Without greeting anyone, Shama picked up a soy taco and stuffed it into her mouth. With the other, she crumbled off a bit of the cake and dropped it in her pocket for Deenay.

The bird abandoned the taco shell and right away began pecking at the chocolate cake.

You've got an even bigger sweet tooth than me.

"Who are you?" a beefy girl sitting across the table from her asked.

On Flade Street, Shama and her friends called girls shaped like this a "bumper" after the indestructible xiathium bumpers on all the newest models of lifters.

"Shama," she said.

"I'm Liberty Quence," the beefy girl said. Shama recognized her as the girl with no chin whose seat Shama had kicked earlier.

On Liberty's tray, Shama saw what she figured was the FoodNOW muscle-building meal: hot dogs loaded with protein. Liberty had five of them.

Shama nodded. She finished one soy taco in a few gulps, then picked up the chocolate cake and stuffed as much as she could in her mouth.

You're right, Dee. This is crunchy.

Hearing someone behind her, she glanced over her shoulder and spotted Gleer Rodriquez.

"May I sit here?" Gleer asked in a small, uncertain voice.

"Sure," Deza said.

Gleer pulled out her chair, set down her plate of vegetable pellets and introduced herself to the table.

Shama's mouth was too full to tell Gleer her name.

Liberty cocked her head in Shama's direction. She said, "That's Shama," as she headed back to FoodNOW.

So it was O.K. to get seconds, Shama thought excitedly.

Gleer had barely set down her tray when, as though she had been asked, she launched into her background. "I live in Upper Philadelphia and go to Ace Catholic. I have two brothers. I'm the youngest…"

Totally uninterested in the girl's story, Shama was about to return to FoodNOW and order a second slice of chocolate cake when Liberty arrived.

Liberty placed a thin box in front of Shama.

Curious, Shama read:

MRE

ALL SELECTIONS COMPLETELY BIODEGRADABLE
WITHIN FIFTEEN MINUTES OF OPENING.
CONTENTS CHECKED BY UNIT THREE,
FIRST DIVISION, THIRD BATTALION.

"What's this?"

"Food," Liberty said, taking her seat again. "MREs. Meals Ready to Eat."

Shama flipped the latch in front and lifted the lid. The food, which was flat like a map, rose above the box, a colorful pop-up. "Whoa!" she said.

Liberty laughed. "Meals Really Evil."

"Compressed food is amazing," Gleer said.

Shama gazed down at the open box. It was a jackpot of lumpy brown applesauce, white potatoes and dark brown pork ribs. Another miracle: the pork ribs and potatoes were warm. She read the instructions: Transport will activate heating salts but to insure a hot meal, probe entrée with fork. Forks and knives lay in a compartment next to the food.

"The DOD sends us thousands of them every year," Liberty said. "At the end of the year, the kitchen just throws all the MREs away." She smirked at Shama. "You looked hungry enough to eat one."

"Why throw them away?" Shama asked. She couldn't imagine throwing away food. She pinched off a bit of potato and dropped it into her pocket for Dee. But the bird ignored the new tidbit, concentrating on the chocolate cake.

"I don't know if it's the compression or the chemicals. But compressed food doesn't taste good. So nobody wants to eat it," Peke said, as he sat down across from Shama.

"You guys are spoiled," Shama said. *And so are you, Deenay.*

Deza puckered her thin lips. Tiny wrinkles creased Gleer's smooth brow. Peke laughed. Liberty watched Shama with amusement.

"Eat it," Liberty dared her.

"You're not going to like it, Shama," Deza said.

Shama stuck her fork into the potatoes and poked it around. She touched the ribs again and found that miraculously the meat felt hot.

She dipped her spoon into the applesauce. Smelling it, she pictured a whole apple tree blooming. But when she put the applesauce in her mouth, the smell vanished. Applesauce ought to slide down her throat, but this stuff moved at a gluey chug. *Not the greatest*, she thought. Still, she'd eaten worse. Often.

She looked up and found the others studying her.

"Crunchy," she said.

As if on cue, they all laughed.

Shama shrugged.

"So what's your word for 'great'?"

"Humid," Liberty said.

"Icy," Deza said.

"Great," Gleer said.

"*Glory. Glory. All hail us brave and strong.*" Without warning the World Nations anthem blared from every square inch of the auditorium.

Deenay stopped eating.

That's music. Don't be afraid.

Shama stuck her hand inside her pocket to calm the bird, but Deenay pinched her finger.

What now?

But Shama answered her own question. Deenay was thirsty. Shama had forgotten to give her water.

She took a chip of ice out of her drink and dropped it into her pocket.

Deenay started pecking on the cold lump.

When Shama looked up, she was surprised to see pink, brown, yellow and red stars lighting up the sky. As the stars began blinking off and on, Liberty hooted. Peke stamped his feet. Gleer and Deza clapped.

"What's this?" Shama asked.

Liberty looked curiously at her. "Holofireworks."

High winds buffeted the tall-ceilinged room, and colorful holostreamers gusted and billowed toward the floor. Hundreds of thousands of white holocandles with bright orange flames lit up around the domed ceiling. The last stanza of the song blared out of the sound system, *From Land to Ocean Bottom to Sky City, Are We...*and the white holocandles—flames and all—and the pink, brown, yellow and red holostreamers began melting. Bits of colored light, red, orange, purple and pink, started raining down.

Shama pointed at the glittering droplets. "Snow?" she asked Liberty.

"Girl, you don't know anything, do you?" Liberty said. "That's holoconfetti."

Shama held out her hand, and the pieces of light passed through her fingers. It was more amazing than an urban trash war. Or the way the UpCity lights made the dust glow during a windstorm. More amazing than anything she had ever seen—except her bird. Which she had made very happy. She could feel Deenay grooming her feathers. A clean bird!

"So where are you from?" Peke said. When he scratched his close-shaven head, it made a sound like sandpaper.

"Lower D.C.," Shama said.

Deza's eyes bugged out even more than usual. Liberty

swallowed her hot dog. Gleer's green eyes filled with curiosity.

"Really?" Peke said. "You don't go to teleschool, do you?"

"Yep," Shama answered, and they all gaped at her as if she were that new breed of talking snake.

"I've never met a teleschool kid before," Peke said.

Liberty rolled her eyes and said, "How did you get admitted?"

"I don't know. I just did," Shama said, taking her last bite of applesauce.

"Leave her alone," Gleer said. "I'm sure it was flade."

Shama looked at Gleer in surprise. "How'd you know? That's the name of my street."

"The name of your street?" Liberty said.

"Are you serious?" Peke said.

Shama shrugged. "What else is flade besides a street?" She took another bite of rib meat and tried to ignore the gooey texture.

Deza answered, "Flade means: Fate. Luck. Destiny. It was coined by the philosopher Hanz Fisher to describe the intersection of predestined time and free will. Chronos uses it to mean…"

Liberty laughed. "You would know that if you had listened to General Mungo's lecture on Time Fundamentalism…"

"I listened," Shama said.

"*You* were asleep. *I* was sitting behind you…" Deza said.

The sound system crackled.

Dean Perbile, the four stars on his beret glittering, stood in the middle of the stage. Behind him, the other teachers put down their glasses and gazed respectfully in his direction. "Cadets! Assemble at the rotunda for a tour. Cadets Jearns, Milersboat, Rearshank and Katooee report to my office."

Liberty turned to Shama. "What does he want you for?"

"He said I have some missing records." Shama shrugged. "Or something like that."

Gleer shuddered. "I think his Wander Eye is awful. I've never seen one of those before."

"The guards at Teen Jail have them," Shama said.

All of them laughed.

"What?" Shama said.

They laughed again.

Chairs scraped the floor. Suddenly, everyone was standing, gathering their things.

Shama didn't move. She had noticed something strange. Her MRE started to dissolve. One corner had disintegrated into blue foam.

Liberty leaned over Shama's shoulder. She smelled like soy grease. "Disgusting, isn't it?" she said. "Like the box says, 'Biodegradable in fifteen minutes.'"

"Urgh!" Shama said, as she watched the pork bones burp blue bubbles.

You were right, Dee. I shouldn't have eaten that stuff.

From her pocket, she heard a tiny *tweet* in reply.

NEW YORK CITY
SEPTEMBER 11, 2001
6:17 A.M.

Maye dipped her spoon into the brown oatmeal and took a bite. The strong dose of cinnamon stung her nose.

"Are you excited about the field trip?" Dan asked as he walked over to the counter.

"Yes," Maye said.

The field trip to the Twin Towers. And for no reason, Maye pictured a fiery red head with melting yellow eyes.

"It's good you're awake early."

Maye looked up at his rust-colored face. She was glad that his voice had stopped her thoughts from sliding back into her nightmare.

"I'm taking a client to breakfast." Dan started piling the loose papers inside his briefcase with the sticker on the side, George Robertson Insurance Agency. "Unless you need anything, I've got to go to work."

Maye shook her head—too hard. She patted her hair to make sure it still hid her ear.

Dan stopped in the doorway. "We're here for you, if you ever want to talk."

Maye stood and took her bowl to the sink. "What about?"

Chronos Academy
UPCITY D.C.
2083
1430 HOURS

"I'm Lieutenant Bazel."

The man speaking to the cadets assembled in a circle had exactly the same stooped posture, pocked skin and hollow eyes as the holoman who brought her to the Academy. But there were differences. The holoman's hair had been combed while Bazel's cap seemed to float on an unruly mop. The holoman's uniform had been neat while the real Bazel's belt was too long and hung down like a tongue.

"I'm going to take you on an Academy tour," Bazel said.

The words "Academy tour" echoed around the hollow rotunda. *It's so big*, Shama thought. So big that Deenay could fly around and maybe no one would see the bird. But she didn't dare take the chance.

Later, Shama promised Dee. She felt the bird's wings lift up and down in a sigh.

Gleer sidled up to Shama. "I thought Dean Perbile called you to his office."

Shama didn't want to miss the tour of the building. She had a question that she needed to answer. How could she leave the Academy and return to Flade Street, if things didn't work out? "I'll go later," she said.

Gleer stepped away from Shama—fast. The expression on her face made Shama want to laugh.

"Before we visit our park, known as the Sim—and a very fine simulated outdoor environment it is, if I do say so myself—we're going to view some of our classrooms," Bazel said. "A number marks each of our twelve hallways. Look on the ground near the entrance, and you'll see it."

Where was the door to the outside?

Although Shama had tried to pay attention when she entered the Academy, now she found the long dimly lit hallways all looked the same.

Deenay, do you know?

When Dee only sighed again, Shama asked, "Which hallway leads to the exit?" Bazel picked Shama out of the crowd. "Cadet Katooee, I believe."

"Yes," Shama said. He said Shama's name precisely, carefully.

Liberty and Deza's eyes fixed on Shama, surprised that the Lieutenant knew her name, and for an instant Shama felt herself puff up.

Did you hear that, Deenay? He knows us. We are supposed to be here.

Dee just curled into a ball.

Bazel turned and pointed across the rotunda. "Most of our traffic with the outside world takes place at night, but it just so happens that you can see someone exiting the indoor/outdoor portal right now."

Shama looked to where Bazel pointed. From this distance, it appeared as if the man in the tan uniform passed through the solid glass wall and disappeared.

"That's Spoke 3," Bazel said.

"Thanks," Shama said.

*We need to be prepared, Dee, in case...*She didn't want to scare the baby bird so she finished with...*you never know.*

"Any other questions?" Bazel said to the group.

Shama wanted to ask, "What's the code for the door?" but she figured this wasn't a question that she could either ask or expect him to answer.

The lump that Deenay made in her pocket felt looser, and she guessed that Dee was falling asleep.

Sleep tight, little bird.

"About this QuanTime machine?" Peke said. He drummed his fingers against his chest as if he still played with his musicblender. "What are we going to watch first?"

Around Shama, the kids erupted in laughter and conversation.

"I'd like to see cowboys."

"Not me. I'd like to watch the colonization of the moon."

"I want to see General Patton during World War II."

"Ah," Bazel said. "65 million years ago an asteroid hit Earth, and the atmosphere became so hot that it quickly incinerated any unprotected life. We call such a moment a reset button, because organic life started over again. During training, you'll watch a segment of time immediately before that asteroid hit. Since carbon-based life is about to get destroyed, nothing we do could possibly affect history."

Without thinking, Shama burst out, "Then we can ride the dinosaurs, right? They're going to be destroyed so what difference would it make?"

Bazel's expression stayed serious. "Good question, Cadet Katooee."

His gaze lingered on Shama, and she felt her face grow warm with embarrassment.

"According to Chronos, we should never be more than mere observers of history." Bazel's tone lacked conviction, as if he were quoting scripture he didn't believe.

Tres stepped out in front of the other students. "What's 'according to Chronos' supposed to mean?" she asked.

Shama had to give it to Tres. She was the only kid who acted unafraid around the teachers. Of course, she was the General's daughter.

"I don't disagree with the Constant of Suffering, Cadet Mungo, not at all. It is absolutely true when applied to cataclysmic events. But some of us on the Command Staff think that if we can figure out a way to help random individuals, we ought to do it," Bazel said. As he spoke these last words, his eyes sought out Shama again.

"Random individuals?" Tres asked. She had placed her hands on her hips in a way that seemed to challenge everything the Lieutenant said. She didn't seem to notice that his gaze passed through her and landed on Shama.

"Think about all the human beings in history who could use our help," Bazel said.

To avoid Bazel's gaze, Shama stared at her new fancy boots and remembered her mother. It would be so great to see her again. Not just on some machine. She longed to fold her arms around her mother's thin body.

When Shama looked up, she was relieved to find that Bazel's attention had shifted to Tres.

"My father." Tres cleared her throat. "I mean General Mungo said...we can't use the QuanTime to help people. That we're just supposed to watch history."

"That's why he teaches Time Fundamentalism, and I teach Time Design. They are opposing theories of Time Management." Bazel smiled a lopsided grin. It seemed to be sad and happy at the same time. Turning his back on Tres, he headed down the hall.

Shama overheard Tres say to Kardo, "I'm going to tell my father what Bazel just said."

"Bazel's an officer and a senior professor at the Academy, Tres," Kardo said. "He's entitled to a different opinion."

Tres just gnawed at the finger in her mouth.

As Shama started walking, she expected Deenay to wake up. But when the bird stayed fast asleep, she figured: *my pocket is a bird cradle.*

"Just for fun, let's take a peek at our most notorious classroom, Stress Adaptation and Management," Bazel said. He stopped walking in front of a glass wall.

"Do first-years have to take it?" Kardo asked.

"No. SAM is a fifth-year class," said the Lieutenant.

Along with the rest of the cadets, Shama peered into an empty room. It had a plain hololaser projector hanging from the ceiling, and sayings written in bold black ink on the glass walls:

PAIN IS WEAKNESS LEAVING THE BODY.

PAIN IS TOO PAINFUL TO WASTE.

CLARITY IS A GIFT OF PAIN.

"There's nothing to see," Liberty complained.

"Precisely," Lieutenant Bazel said. "Pain and discomfort are in your mind."

"I'm already dreading this class," Gleer whispered to Shama.

"This class is going to be easy for me. Things in my *mind* don't hurt," Liberty boasted.

Liberty looked strong, but since she had grown up in the Zone, an invisible glass house, she couldn't have fought often or hard.

"So what *do* you think hurts?" Shama asked. She was really curious.

Liberty looked at her.

"A broken bone. A punch in the gut. A slap to the head… you know, physical stuff."

"Have you ever got hit by a pain beam?"

"Are you crazy?" Liberty said. "We don't have weapons here."

"I got caught in the middle of a Flay war once. A pain beam grazed my stomach," Shama said.

"Ouch!" Liberty winced.

Bazel was talking again, gesturing at the empty classroom.

"Using our artificial weather system, we can stage rain, snow, lightning and thunder. With a push of the button, we can make this room a frigid 60 below or a torrid 130 degrees."

"That's even hotter than Lower D.C.," Shama said. Once Shama had had to walk about ten kilometers in the desert around Lower D.C. without water. Her mother had called her "a camel."

"How many of you are excited about taking Stress Management in your fifth year?" Lieutenant Bazel asked.

Shama looked around at the kids, at the furrowed foreheads, the frowns, the pursed lips. Tres appeared thoughtful. Gleer had turned two shades lighter. Liberty flexed the muscles in her biceps as if trying to get herself ready. No one raised a hand.

The Academy has to teach cadets about pain and survival! They should send them to live on Flade Street, Shama thought. She couldn't help feeling a little proud.

You and I are tough, Deenay.

But she didn't feel any answering tug on her thoughts. Her tough baby bird was still asleep.

"I'm Colonel Pink-Branch."

The man greeting the cadets as they entered their first-period class was short compared with the rest of the colonels—under two meters—and had a wide smile and tiny ears. His thick brown hair flipped up in a few places, but especially in the back where one hefty chunk curled out from under his cap.

Shama recognized him as the man she had seen talking to Bazel in the auditorium and again in the Mess Hall. "The cadets call me Pinkie," he said to the class. Grinning, he added, "But not to my face."

Pinkie strode over to the machine against the wall. "Time to get started." He reached out and touched the machine. "This is a Master Operational Gaming Theatre." He smiled. "Nickname: the mixer."

The mixer took up half of the far wall. It was a nondescript box with a control panel of buttons and dials.

Pinkie began pointing at the buttons and reciting their functions: 3-D, odor, color, animation, maximize, minimize...Shama had never seen a mixer before, and she was impressed.

"For your assignment," Pinkie said. "I want you to draw a person, someone who is important in your life. It can be anyone." He pointed at the long table in the center of the room, bare except for a pile of dataplates and styluses. "I want you to have fun with your first holodesign."

"Like we can have fun when we know we're being tested," Liberty said, in a whisper loud enough to be heard by everybody in the room.

A smile played on Pinkie's lips, appearing, disappearing, returning even brighter. "Since we're just creating a rudimentary hologram, after you've drawn your picture, we'll skip several steps, and I'll show you how to enhance your drawing. I doubt any of you will be able to create a 3-D figure in" —he glanced at his communicator—"two hours. But give it your best shot."

Tres pushed past Shama in a dash to the table.

Pinkie called out, "At the end of class, we'll model some of your designs." He sat down on a stool by the door. "Begin."

At teleschool, Shama was used to everyone wasting as much time as they could. *These kids seem like they had just started a race*, Shama thought as she watched the cadets claim places around the drawing table.

By the time Shama grabbed a corner stool—the only empty one left—next to Tres, the girl was already using her stylus to draw on the dataplate, as if she had prepared for this assignment all her life.

Shama wanted to draw Deenay and show her bird the picture when she woke up, but that wouldn't be smart. "Hide the bird," the holoman had said. Instead, she decided to draw her mother. She drew a stick figure, skinny arms, legs and a round bubble head. Her mother had been thin... but not that thin.

Her mother wore her long gray hair in a ponytail. But since the stick figure faced Shama, how could she show a ponytail on the back of the figure's head? Instead, she drew spikes raying out of the top. Then she thickened the spikes until they looked wild, sort of like her own hair. She tried to think about what her mother's face had looked like. She remembered her light brown eyes, the bump in the middle of her nose, her soft mouth. But she didn't know how to draw that.

She squeezed her eyes tight and forced herself to remember.

Her house slippers! When her mother bought them, the shoes were pink and covered in downy fluff like a chick's feathers. But they had turned gray, and the fluff had worn off, leaving a tough, dimpled fabric, so well-worn that her mother said they were her second pair of feet. Shama still kept them in the box underneath her cot in the room behind Poppers. The shoes would be easier to draw than her mother's face.

Shama sketched the stick figure's feet, but her mother's house slippers were wide and flat, and the shoes she had drawn came out narrow and long. They looked like minia-ture caskets, not a pair of slippers.

She glanced at her own tan shoes. They were plain, and the ionic clasp that bound the two sides of the shoe together was smooth, almost invisible. Only a bit of red ribbing along the edges stood out and gave the shoes any flair.

She enabled the color function on her dataplate and selected red. On each side of the figure's boxy-looking shoes, she drew a red line to represent the ribbing. She reselected black and outlined her mother's favorite long T-shirt over the thin body. The one Shama used to wear every night.

Shama colored the T-shirt light blue and began lettering the saying that was on her mother's T-shirt: *Chips are a Complete Nutritional Meal.* But she didn't space the slogan right, and she ran out of space after *Nut…*

She thought about what else she could draw. Red welts covered her mother's hands from mending clothes made out of Breathe fabric, but Shama wasn't about to draw those burned hands. She didn't even like thinking about them.

All around her, the cadets had their heads bent over their artwork, and for the first time since she had been in the UpCity, she smelled sweat.

Pinkie looked up from his communicator, and she raised her hand to get his attention. He stood up and walked to Shama's station. She pointed at her drawing. "That's the best I can do."

"Not bad. Not bad," Pinkie said. "Who is it?"

She didn't want to insult her mother so she said, "It's me."

"These aren't supposed to be masterpieces. Just experiments," Pinkie said. "Try to draw a face."

"I don't know how," Shama protested.

"Just try," Pinkie urged her.

Her mother had broken her nose, and it was bent near the top. She didn't pick up the stylus but drew a sideways nose with her finger. She added a bump in the middle. A witch's nose.

"Now, some eyes," Pinkie said.

Her mother's eyes were light brown, really golden, with tiny wrinkles radiating out from the sides. She tried but the eyes she drew resembled two yellow slits. Evil eyes.

"And a mouth."

She just drew a straight line. A stern mouth.

The drawing looked nothing at all like her mother.

Pinkie cupped his chin in his hand. "Not to worry. We know our cadets all have different strengths and weaknesses," he said. "Perhaps you'd like to pass the remaining time in our library viewing other student work."

Shama was glad to leave her drawing and to follow Pinkie, whose renegade tuft of hair waved back and forth as he walked.

He passed a water fountain, a smaller FoodNOW that said snacks only, and a vitajuice dispenser before he stopped at a room full of holofigures in all shapes, types and sizes: a frog with camel legs; a bird with the colonel's head; a monk wearing roller blades; a tree with an elevator in its trunk; a bowl full of heads, and on and on. A sign hanging from the ceiling said:

LIBRARY OF ZONE HOLOGRAMS—STUDENT PRODUCTIONS

Shama pointed at the rows packed with colorful shapes. "Cadets made these?"

"We've saved all our classes' designs since the Zone opened in 2061," Pinkie said.

Shama heard the classroom doors retract and looked up to investigate. She recognized Lieutenant Bazel.

Pinkie followed Shama's gaze.

"Ahh," he said. "My esteemed colleague."

Dipping his head toward Shama, he said, "Excuse me. Feel free to explore."

She watched Pinkie return to the front and greet Lieutenant Bazel. They walked to a corner of the lab, and their heads bent together in conversation. The two colonels were too far away to eavesdrop, so, with nothing better to do, she turned her attention to the student designs.

A toilet with wings.

A fireman with water pouring out of his head.

A lamp with gills.

A tree standing on its head.

A fork with a pig on each prong.

Next, she stumbled onto a whole section labeled Doile Perbile, Dean of Chronos Academy. A few kids had colored his entire face yellow. Others had poked fun at his Wander Eye.

One version had modeled Dean Perbile's features on Prominent Design—*Faces that inspire trust!*—a favorite look of judges and politicians, who paid big credit coins to have their faces reengineered.

At least in teleschool, kids couldn't flatter the teleteachers.

After what seemed only a few minutes, Pinkie called out, "Cadets! It's time! Now we'll model some of your designs." He rubbed his hands together with excitement. "Cadet Mungo."

Tres stood. "I didn't have time to finish," she protested.

Pinkie grinned. "I don't know if the General told you but during Orientation, many of the tests are psychological, not skill based." He brushed a hand through the air as if to drive away their worries. "You needn't worry about your drawing ability."

Shama heard a low rumble of complaints.

"What does that mean? Psychological tests?" Deza murmured.

Pinkie said, "Cadet Mungo, please, bring your drawing to the mixer."

Tres stepped up to the front of the classroom. The speckles on her cheeks had turned bright red. "It's not good."

Pinkie took Tres' dataplate from her. "No worries. Just pretend that today our only goal is to get a feel of the equipment." He plugged her dataplate into the dock.

"Who did you draw?" Pinkie asked.

"My father," Tres said.

"Another drawing of our esteemed General," Pinkie said. "He'll be delighted."

Tres' portrait appeared in front of the mixer. It wasn't 3-D, only one-dimensional. The figure was really tall. His face was a complete blank; she hadn't filled it in, only drawn a gray cape around his shoulders. His feet were a few meters above the ground, and his toes were pointed and his arms raised, as if he were landing.

Somehow, the drawing looked like a magical General Mungo.

"Father Time," Kardo said.

What a great nickname for General Mungo, Shama thought.

Peke let out a low whistle. "That's good."

"Why'd you draw him that way?" Liberty said.

"He gave some lectures once where he wore a cape," Tres said.

Kardo said, "Your drawing is great, Tres."

Gleer's portrait of Pinkie had no hands, arms, feet or eyes and only one half of a smile. But the Colonel's slight trunk, small ears, downturned nose and telltale tuft of hair were, as Shama would expect from Gleer, perfect: detailed and realistic.

"Thank you, Cadet Rodriquez, for the fetching portrait," Pinkie said.

Deza hadn't attempted to draw a face, "I'm just good at bodies," she said. But what a body. Deza had drawn her own full chest, tiny waist and long legs. "This is a self-portrait."

Kardo had sketched his little sister, Graciella. The girl looked to be about seven or eight with long dark hair and pink cheeks. Her mouth was wide open. Kardo explained, "Graciella talks all the time."

Pinkie said, "Wonderful. Wonderful. I can tell this is going to be a great class of young cadets. Such talent."

Lieutenant Bazel sat quietly, just watching. A few times, he seemed to try to catch Shama's eye, but unsure what he wanted from her, she looked away.

"Cadet Katooee, I don't believe we've seen yours," Pinkie said. "Cadet Katooee's is wonderfully playful."

Shama reached her dataplate, still on the table where she had left it. When she looked down, she saw to her horror that next to it, a cup lay on its side. A puddle of liquid covered the screen. Frantically, she drained it into the cup and brushed off the extra moisture with her hand. Examining the dataplate, she found, as she had feared, that the lines of her design had blurred and smeared. Shadows bruised the drawing's face.

As Shama walked up to the front, she rubbed her drawing against her leg. "Someone spilled water on it."

Pinkie plugged in Shama's design dataplate. When her stick figure appeared in the empty space in front of the mixer, Shama gasped.

Maximized, the figure was as tall as she was. Not only was the original outline of the figure crude and thick, but it had smeared into smoke. Her mother's eyes, nose and mouth had become blackened cuts. The red on the sides of the shoes rose up as if her feet were flames. Her mother looked as if she was burning.

Titters and giggles spread throughout the room. Shama felt sick.

Colonel Pink-Branch's gaze swept the room. "Whose cup is that on the table?"

The kids all turned and stared at the lone white cybratom cup. No one answered.

"I like practical jokes, but I will not tolerate a mean joke in my class," Pinkie said. For the first time, his voice was hard with disapproval.

Shama looked straight at Tres.

Tres had pressed her lips together and wouldn't raise her eyes.

Shama shoved her way through the crowd of cadets and started for the door.

NEW YORK CITY
SEPTEMBER 11, 2001
7:04 A.M.

Crossing at the light, Maye jogged toward St. Pius Catholic School.

Sister Rose waited in front of the statue of St. Peter. Dressed in a full black- and-white habit, Maye's principal had dark hair that curled out of her headpiece and softened her square face. Although from this distance Maye couldn't see the Sister's black eyes, from experience she knew they never missed anything.

Maye rushed up to Sister Rose. "I'm sorry, Sister. It's not my fault. My bus was late." As she combed her fingers through her hair, she endured Sister Rose's gaze. It started at her black tennis shoes and traveled up her legs to the jagged edge of her blue uniform skirt. Maye had hemmed it herself. Sister Rose's gaze rose to Maye's eyes.

Maye said, "May I go, Sister?"

"Did you say your prayers this morning, Maye?" Sister Rose said.

"Yes, ma'am," Maye lied. She saw no point in praying.

Sister Rose turned and waved at the students in the white St. Pius van. It had already begun pulling away. "You make your life harder than it needs to be, Maye Jones."

"Yes, ma'am." Maye readied herself for the worst. A day in the classroom, alone with Sister Rose.

While the cars crawled past on 17th Street, she studied Sister Rose's expression, waiting. Sister Rose's dark eyes and broad nose looked normal one minute. Then—in a pattern that was becoming familiar—in the next, the air in front of Sister Rose began rippling, and Sister Rose's profile grew wavy.

Maye blinked hard and felt grateful when Sister Rose came back into focus.

"You may go," Sister Rose said.

Every once in a while even I *get a break*, Maye thought as she said, "Thank you, Sister Rose."

Maye turned toward the second van, older than Maye. It had St. Pius Catholic School written in big letters on its sides.

"The vans are full," Sister Rose said. "You can ride with Mr. Fussman."

"Mr. Fussman?" Maye said. St. Pius' cranky handyman.

Sister Rose countered the note of complaint in Maye's voice with her own even tone, "Yes. Mr. Fussman."

So the day was messed up after all. Reluctantly, Maye headed toward the beat-up black car.

Chronos Academy
UPCITY D.C.
2083
1634 HOURS

In an Observation Station, Shama sat on a bench facing the fading sun. She didn't care that Deenay was still asleep. She woke the bird up and set it on her shoulder.

I need you.

Shama felt Deenay's claws grip her shirt. The bird began to hop on one foot, then the other.

Wake-up exercises?

The second bell rang. Time Fitness had begun. Even if she wanted to, Shama couldn't race, hang from a rope or do whatever exercises Chronos thought were important. All she could think about was Tres. "I want to beat that girl up. Make her look as sad and terrible as Mama did."

The bird let out a soft chirp.

"You can talk," Shama said, delighted. Then she thought of the "Stay as inconspicuous as possible" advice.

I hope you don't talk too much.

Deenay chirped a little louder this time.

Shama heard footsteps approaching. When she looked over her shoulder, she saw Lieutenant Bazel. His hooded eyelids matched the color of the air, a bruised blue.

Shama groaned and studied her shoes.

"May I join you?" he said.

"Why did you bring me here?" Shama demanded.

Bazel glanced at Deenay, and Shama expected him to tell her to put the bird up. But Bazel surprised her by asking, "Do you mind if I give you a long answer?"

Shama shrugged. She wasn't ready to go back to class.

"I was born, well before the launch of the UpCities, a heavy child—thirteen pounds at birth, but otherwise not remarkable."

Bazel said the words, otherwise not remarkable, in a way that implied that he became remarkable fast.

Deenay began stringing chirps together.

Although Shama reached up and patted Deenay's top-knot, she forced herself to listen to Bazel.

"I watched teleschool with all the other toddlers and learned to read and write. My favorite teleschool teacher was Radar III. We were told that her radar eyes could see us, and I absolutely believed they could."

Shama thought about her own favorite teleschool teacher. When Radar XXVII said, "You are such good students," Shama always felt proud. Now, Shama knew that Radar XXVII taught a class of millions.

"I never knew who my mother was. I never asked. It was just my father, Looray Bazel and me. Before the Zone was constructed, Chronos was housed in a lab in Lower D.C. For fifteen years, my father was the robot-maintenance supervisor there.

Chirp. Chirp. Chirp.

Are you trying to tell me something?

Chirp.

"At the Orientation this morning, you heard General

Mungo talk about the man who invented the QT?" Bazel asked.

Shama couldn't remember the inventor's name, but she nodded.

"My father got to know Dr. Lassemar this way. My father saw a robotic maid about to g-pipe a pair of shoes that the robot had found in his trashcan. They looked perfectly good to my father. Although my father retrieved them and put them back on Lassemar's desk, that night he found them headed for the g-pipe again. He repeated the process. The next day, Lassemar came to the robotic cleaning closet where my father took his breaks and asked for the person who wouldn't let the robots throw away a pair of old shoes. After that, the two men talked often. My father even thought they were friends."

Shama noticed that Bazel's voice had grown bitter.

"The first superpox epidemic began in a remote town in the East Asia District. I can still remember hearing about the spread of the disease from the squawkers." He roughened his voice, mimicking a squawkcaster's as he repeated, "'A new microorganism may be growing in your drinking water. Normal sterilization techniques are not sufficient to kill it. Use extreme caution. Impure water is the carrier of a deadly disease called superpox.'" He paused, then continued, "I'm sure you know that millions of people died before the vaccine was available."

Shama touched the scar on her upper arm. She had been vaccinated for superpox when she was just a little girl. She remembered clearly that the shot had hurt.

Chirp. Chirp. Chirp.

If you chirp in class, I'm going to have to fake a coughing spell. So, sing all you want here, but then quiet, O.K.?

Although the bird was silent, Shama knew exactly what she was thinking: *I'll talk when I want to talk.*

Shama practiced a loud cough, just in case.

Bazel didn't notice. "The East Asia District seemed a long way off but we too got our water from the oceans," he continued. "Before I knew it, a superpox epidemic swept Lower D.C., and I was no longer able to leave our one-room apartment.

"My father didn't let me watch the imagetube often, and I didn't know what superpox looked like until my father came home from work one day. As you know, the disease progresses quickly." He sat there, not saying anything for a while.

"I was lucky."

Shama pictured a young Bazel shut up alone with his father's body.

I'm not so sure about that.

Chirp. Chirp.

"By the time Lassemar arrived at my door, I was infected. One glance at the apartment told him how I had been living. Although I'm about to tell you his flaws, Lassemar wasn't a monster, and he made sure that I got the treatment I needed. A lucky few recover from superpox, and I was one of the survivors. Afterwards, Lassemar enrolled me at the school for the sons and daughters of Chronos' scientists. At that time, he was the Dean of the Academy. I was way behind the other students, but where else could I go?"

Shama nodded.

Bazel remained silent for several minutes.

Deenay began climbing Shama's hair like it was a ladder.

As Shama pulled Dee out of her hair and set the bird back on her shoulder, Bazel turned to her and said, "I know what you're dreaming about."

Shama just looked at him.

"I, too, fantasized about figuring out some way to use the QuanTime to save my parent," Bazel said.

"Is that possible?"

"I tried."

"What happened?"

"Only two weeks after my father died," Bazel continued, "the President announced the discovery of a vaccine for superpox."

He sighed.

"This haunted me for years. Everything would have been different if my father had stayed healthy for just a few more weeks. After I found out about the QuanTime, I reasoned that if Chronos could go back and *watch* history as it unfolded, maybe I could find a way to break through. I promised myself that I would save my father. No matter the Fundamentalist propaganda that I was learning at the Academy. No matter the consequences."

Dee flew off her shoulder and landed on the bench. She paced the space between Shama and Bazel.

"I know what you mean," Shama said to Bazel. She had been thinking about her mother a lot since she'd heard the General talk about the lens that could see the past.

"I passed the tests during Orientation week, got admitted to the Academy and worked very hard. In fact, I became a star student. Eventually in my advanced classes, I learned how to program the QuanTime," Bazel said. One side of his mouth rose as if he were trying to smile. "I was entrusted with Chrono's access codes during my fifth year at the Academy."

Dee flew from the bench over to the fake grass lawn.

Stay where I can see you.

Deenay immediately disappeared, her green topknot camouflaged by the grass.

"On my own, I worked out the mathematical formula necessary for me to calculate the coordinates that would enable me to watch my father the week before he got ill."

"What happened?"

"Back then, only a series of passwords protected the QuanTime at night. One night I stood in front of the QuanTime, hoping that all my hard work was about to pay off. You'll see—it's a remarkable device. Once the complicated coordinates are entered, traveling to a segment in history only requires the push of a button. However, in this case, when I pushed, nothing happened."

As Bazel said these words, his finger jabbed softly the air, and Shama could tell that even years later he could still feel that button. "I pushed it again and again, I don't know how many times. Before long, Lassemar entered the room."

"I thought you said the QuanTime wasn't guarded," Shama said.

"It wasn't," said Bazel. "But everyone in the compound was watched constantly. They had been tracking me, and when I entered the access codes, they shut down the QuanTime."

Shama grunted.

Bazel smiled at her. "You know the way adults look at you when they are very disappointed?"

Shama nodded. *Of course.*

"That's how Lassemar looked. He said, 'I didn't expect this from you.'"

Shama imagined a young Lieutenant Bazel in trouble, with Lassemar, his Dean, standing over him.

"He said to me, 'You're trying to save your father, aren't you?'"

Bazel almost smiled at Shama. "I was dumbfounded that I had been so obvious." But when he looked at her next, with lids half-closed, Shama sensed he had come to the most painful part of his story.

"Lassemar said, 'Young man, we are the guardians of history. Even if the Constant of Suffering weren't a natural law and we could change history to save one life without sacrificing another, we wouldn't start by saving your father.'"

Shama shot bolt upright. "What a Flayhead!"

"That's what I thought, too," Bazel said. "At that moment Lassemar led me to my life's mission."

"What's that?" Shama said.

"Figuring out a way to force Chronos to intervene in history and save individuals' lives," Bazel said.

Shama felt her heart quicken.

"So did you? Can you?"

Bazel looked at her, his face full of sorrow. It took her back to Flade Street, to the nights she had spent hungry there, and she thought, *He does understand.* But then his eyes narrowed and reminded her of Poppers when she was calculating her chances of squeezing more profit out of a deal.

Bazel spoke quickly, as if he needed to get the words out before he changed his mind. "The QuanTime is really a time-*travel* machine."

Shama said, "So Mungo lied?" She wasn't surprised. Adults lied a lot.

"Not lied," Bazel said. "This is Orientation. We don't trust cadets with that information until much later."

The full force of what Bazel had said hit Shama. "So I can save my mother," she said. "Will you show me how?"

"No." Bazel shook his head.

"Why not?" Shama demanded.

"Time is a complicated mix of nodes that can be changed—or areas of free will, if you want to call them that—and lines of predestination that man cannot affect. If Lassemar hadn't stopped me, I would have failed anyway. My father's death is a knot that can't be unraveled," Bazel said.

"I don't understand. What are you saying?"

Bazel scratched his chin. "All right. I see you deserve that, don't you? Besides, we don't have much time."

"So tell me," Shama said.

Bazel's hands clenched and unclenched nervously. "The bird is key."

Shama looked over to the grassy mound where Dee was playing.

That's right, Dee. You're pretty special.

Bazel repeated, "*The* key. The final piece of the puzzle."

Shama interrupted him before he could say more. "What do you mean?"

"No one knows you have the bird, do they?" Bazel said, ignoring her question.

Shama shook her head.

Bazel grunted. "Good."

"So what's going on?"

Bazel said, "Well…" He gulped in air as if taking a drink. "This might seem a little far-fetched to you, but you have to travel back in time."

"I thought you said I couldn't go back and change anything that mattered," Shama said.

"I *said*, the time isn't right for you to rescue your mother." Bazel paused. "But you can help others."

"Why would I do that?" Shama said.

"Because you're a lot like the girl I'm going to introduce you to. You're both strong. You've endured a lot. You're on your own," Bazel said.

Shama rolled her eyes. She shouldn't have come.

Bazel reached over and rested his hand lightly on her knee. "Although we aren't always able to choose the people we can help, we can still save other people's lives."

Shama brushed off his hand. "Who cares," she said. Bitter with disappointment, she stood up.

Come.

A ball of color burst up from the grass and soared toward Shama.

"Shama," Bazel said. "I have something to show you! If Dean Perbile corners you about your missing records, stall him for a few days. It will be easy to do."

"Why?" Shama said.

We need to go!

She heard a whizz near her ear and knew that Deenay was with her.

"Come see me during Assembly tomorrow, and I'll explain more. No one will notice that you're not there," Bazel called after her. "And for God's sake, put up and SHUT UP that bird."

At dinner in the Mess Hall, Shama found Kardo and Tres sitting at the far table. And by the look on Tres' face, she guessed that the two were arguing.

That was fine with Shama. She intended to argue with Tres, too.

Holding her loaded tray, Shama stood behind an empty chair and met Tres' glare. "You can apologize any time."

Tres squirmed and looked down at her tray.

"My drawing," Shama insisted.

"I spilled some water." Tres shrugged and met Shama's gaze for the first time. "An accident." She paused. "I swear it."

Kardo put his hand on the top of the chair and said to Shama, "You want to sit down?"

Shama held Tres' gaze and smiled. "I accept your apology." She pulled out the chair and seated herself.

Tres thrust away her plate of untouched vegetable pellets. "We were in the middle of a serious discussion." She paused. "You always put other people before me, Kardo." She stood up. "I *told* you how that makes me feel." She stormed off.

Shama opened her mouth wide and bit off a huge

hunk of a cartura—a blend of carrot, turnip, and apple. Crunchy. After checking that Kardo's attention was fixed on Tres' retreating figure, she took a bit of the white meat and dropped it into her pocket.

Shama could feel Deenay pecking the crumb.

Better than worm, huh?

She turned to Kardo and asked, "What's up with her?"

Kardo shook his head. "I think she just broke up with me."

"I'm sorry."

Kardo popped an orange vegetable pellet into his mouth.

Shama noticed that he didn't look that upset.

"I really like her." Kardo wiped his lips with his cleaner. "But boy, she can be tough." He let out a low whistle.

Chirp. Chirp. Chirp.

The bird had already finished dinner and was demanding more.

Wait. She stuck her hand in her pocket and dropped in another bite of cartura.

But Shama was too late. By the funny look Kardo gave her, she knew he had heard the bird sounds.

"Is that a BriZance?" he asked.

Shama nodded. "You won't tell, will you?" she pleaded.

Kardo grinned. "Never," he said. "I love those birds."

"Excuse me. She has a sweet tooth and wants some cake." Shama pinched off a huge piece and dropped it in her pocket. "Do you have a BriZance?"

"I did," Kardo said. His gray eyes looked sad. "I guess you know they have pretty short life spans."

"No," Shama said. She didn't want to hear any more.

Besides, Deenay was just a baby.

A happy baby. Happily eating her cake.

"My parents wouldn't let me get another one because I was coming to the Academy," Kardo said. "What's your bird's name?"

"Deenay."

"BriZances are the world's first living machine," Kardo said as though she'd asked the question. "BriZances use water and food to fuel their batteries. They're the perfect pet."

"You want to see her?" Shama said.

"Yeah," Kardo said. He stood up and walked around the table. He sat down in the chair next to hers and leaned in close.

Shama drew open the pocket of her tan pants. The BriZance stopped eating and its orange eyes peered up at her. With its dirty beak slightly parted, the bird looked like she was smiling. A kid with chocolate on her face.

When Kardo gazed down at Deenay, his face lit up. "It's beautiful," he said. He stroked the bird's topknot with his thumb.

Deenay's orange eyes grew brighter. She reared back her head and pecked his finger.

"Ouch," Kardo said. His face flushed with embarrassment. "I forgot," he said. "They don't allow anyone to touch them except their owners...because of the bond."

Shama felt proud. Deenay needed her—for more than chocolate cake.

Shama tussled the bird's topknot. "She's just a baby."

"I know how you feel." Kardo looked sadly at her. "And you need to be really careful." He paused. "I don't know what the Command Staff would do if they find out you have her. Dean Perbile is really strict about the no pets rule."

Shama glanced over her shoulder.

Tres stood by the vitabar sipping her juice and glaring at Shama.

"Oh, I'll be careful all right," Shama said.

NEW YORK CITY
SEPTEMBER 11, 2001
7:09 AM.

Maye could see Mr. Fussman clearly in the front seat behind the steering wheel, wearing a black beret. The front passenger's seat was empty.

No way she was going to sit next to Mr. Fussman. All the girls had heard him complain, "You stop up the toilets with your sanitary products..." He never cared if boys were around.

In the back, Angela Duncan clutched a cell phone.

When Maye's hand touched the backseat door handle, her heart skipped a beat. Not because of Angela Duncan. She spotted Victor Bhatt sitting next to the far window.

"Hi, Angela," Maye said cheerfully, but her gaze fixed on Victor. "Hi, Victor," she said more softly.

"Hey, Maye," Victor said.

Angela scooted over to sit in the middle, next to Victor.

Even with Angela between them, Maye felt a thrill as she slid onto the seat and closed the door.

Mr. Fussman turned the key in the ignition. The car coughed and sputtered before it lurched forward.

As Maye buckled up, she looked out the window and saw Sister Rose waving. Then the van merged with the morning traffic, and Sister Rose and St. Pius disappeared.

Chronos Academy
UPCITY D.C.
2083
1941 HOURS

Stuffed after a dinner of soy meat, three carturas, one
piece of chocolate cake and two bowls of ice cream, Shama
set off to explore the Academy, this time without a guide.
With an hour before lights out, she wanted to check out
that exit portal on her own. As she crossed the rotunda,
she heard someone chasing after her. She turned and saw
that it was Gleer. The girl ran slowly, crossing one foot over
the other, her arms shaking loose at her side.

Deenay, she runs like a target.

The bird let out a little chirp.

"May I come with you?" Gleer said.

Her blonde hair curled around her face and framed
green eyes, the color of Deenay's topknot.

Usually, Shama would rather be alone. That way she
might be able to let Deenay out of her pocket. But after two
hunks of chocolate cake, Deenay was too full and lazy to
want to exercise, so she said, "Sure."

Although Gleer seemed an unlikely friend, Shama
sensed that they had something in common. While Shama
felt alone because the other kids were so sheltered, Gleer
stood apart because she was even more innocent than the
rest of the cadets.

"Where are you going?" Gleer asked.

"The exit," Shama confessed. "I may have to get out of here. Fast."

Gleer's green eyes widened with concern.

"What do you mean?"

"Have you ever been in trouble, even once in your life?" Shama asked.

Gleer quickly answered, "No."

Shama tried to imagine hanging out with Gleer on Flade Street, but she couldn't. A girl like Gleer would have to buy one of those personal security cages like Poppers' and stay locked up if she wanted to keep from getting eaten alive.

Across the rotunda, Shama saw other groups of kids fan out to explore different hallways. Passing Spoke 4, they ran into Liberty and a boy named Huelgo Reel. Huelgo was almost as broad as Liberty. Both had biceps that bulged underneath their tan T-shirts. Both swaggered rather than walked.

"We're going to climb up to the Observation Post. Want to go with us?" Liberty called to them.

"Later," Shama said.

"We're looking for the exit," Gleer called out to Liberty and Huelgo. "Shama wants to know…"

Shama nudged Gleer with her elbow.

Gleer looked up at her surprised. "What?" she said.

Shama frowned, and Gleer's mouth clamped closed.

Shama waited to scold her until after Liberty and Huelgo had disappeared down the dark hallway. "Don't tell them my plans."

"Why not?" Gleer said.

"Burn," Shama said. This girl didn't know anything. "Liberty's mother is a teacher. Liberty might say something."

Shama turned away from Gleer's hurt look to examine the circular perimeter of the rotunda. She fixed her attention on a spot midway between Spokes 2 and 4 where a row of 3s lined the wall. No door stood directly over the letters, only a wall.

She moved closer and examined the wall, solid and riddled with bubbles, pale balloons in a glass sky. The key could be a command, a contact point or something even more high-tech. She had no idea how to do it.

"It figures." She kicked the wall. "They blocked it off."

"What do you mean, Shama?" Gleer said.

"The indoor/outdoor portal. They hid the door so we can't get out," Shama said.

"I don't understand. This is a great school. Why would you want to escape?" Gleer said.

Deenay, you're more with it than this girl.

The bird didn't answer. It was taking a postdinner nap.

"Never mind," Shama answered Gleer. "We might as well explore one of these other spokes." She pointed at Spoke 7. "I haven't seen anyone go down there."

They had only taken a couple of steps when Gleer complained, "It's too dark."

Shama didn't slow her pace, just explained, "We're inside a high-security building in UpCity. The spot where we're standing is probably the safest square meter in both worlds." It was too dark to see Gleer's face, but Shama's words must have soothed her because Shama heard the uneven pat of Gleer's feet following behind.

In front of the door to the first classroom, Shama stopped and waited to see whether a microchip would register her presence and let her inside.

The glass panels retreated.

Shama stepped into the classroom.

Gleer hugged the door. "The Dean didn't give us permission to go inside the classrooms."

Shama said, "He said we could explore the Academy, and the doors aren't locked."

Gleer's hands hung limply at her sides. "He meant the building. Not the classrooms," she said. "Did you ever go see him?"

"No," Shama snapped. She wasn't sure what to do now that Bazel had told her to avoid the Dean. Although Bazel had brought her here, she had no reason to trust him either. "Lights," she called out. When the lights flashed on, to her disappointment all she saw was some chairs, a hololaser projector hanging from the ceiling, and a black box stuck on the wall, the controls for the holoimage tube.

Boring.

"Come on in," Shama called to Gleer. "Nothing's in here."

Gleer took a few timid steps inside. "Why didn't you go see Dean Perbile?"

"Because I didn't get around to it," Shama said. She had meant to stop by the Dean's office during Study Hall, but then she had had that conversation with Bazel.

"You should go see him first thing in the morning," Gleer said.

"Maybe I will," Shama said.

"You wouldn't want to get in trouble," Gleer said. "They might kick you out."

That's when it hit Shama. A new worry. What did Chronos do if a kid didn't work out? Perbile couldn't just put her back on Flade Street. She'd been inside the Academy. She knew secrets; Perbile didn't even know all the secrets Shama knew.

Why is everything always so complicated? Shama thought as she opened the box on the wall and studied the rows of buttons and many-colored dials before pushing one labeled program. *This must be a history classroom,* she thought as she scanned the long list on the screen: Roman times, Greek mythology, early American history…It wasn't until she had nearly reached the bottom that she found one that interested her, "Overview of *UpCity Lives*." *UpCity Lives* was her favorite holoimage tube series.

Gleer cleared her throat. "I just remembered I didn't finish my homework." She turned and headed for the door. "I've got to go."

"We have homework?" Shama asked. She had found the program she wanted to watch and searched for the play switch.

"Remember," Gleer said. "Dean Perbile said we're going to have to have a test on four chapters of Time Fundamentalism tomorrow."

That's why Shama had forgotten. She knew she couldn't finish four chapters by tomorrow. Eighty-four pages.

No way, Deenay. Hey, that rhymes.

No response. Still napping.

"Well, I'll see you later," Gleer called.

Shama heard Gleer's footsteps rushing down the glass hallway, so fast it sounded as if she were being chased.

Shama pushed a green button and turned around to check to see if she had managed to activate the program.

A few meters away from her, Pleez—one of the lead characters in the popular series—appeared. His face was an ordinary ball of light brown flesh with a knobbed nose and starved eyebrows over hazel eyes. But she knew from watching the program that his features could twist from joy to rage to anger to laughter in the space of a split second.

She jiggled her pocket.

You ought to see this.

But when Deenay didn't move, Shama decided to let her sleep. The bird was a baby after all. And babies had to sleep if they were going to live for a long time. Forget about what Kardo said.

He doesn't know everything.

Shama settled down to watch the program alone.

Although Shama had watched all the reruns of *UpCity Lives,* she liked the first season best. During episode one, the hundred families who had colonized the UpCities had marketed themselves in a sensational way. A randomizer, with a whole dictionary in its memory, spat out new last names for each family and first names for each individual. On account of the unique naming technique, the GodZillionaires had ended up with unforgettable names worthy of stars on a best-selling holoimage tube series: Shady Realization, Journey Upended, Binge Potato and Last Wrestler, who stood before her now.

Shady Realization had droopy brown eyes and limp brown hair and clutched a gold-plated notebook. Young Shady's hobby was eavesdropping, and she wrote everything she heard down in her journal along with some made-up stories, too. When she read her notes to the audience, Shady never failed to cause an uproar.

Binge Potato, who hugged his blue blanket to his chest, was the brother of Lesser Potato. Lesser was the first and only child to tumble off an UpCity boundary wall and fall to Earth. The tragedy of Lesser's death and the havoc her body caused in Lower New York City had occupied one whole season on *UpCity Lives*.

It was great to see the familiar cast but Shama wanted to activate the program. She had returned to the box and opened the lid when she heard footsteps.

Kardo stood in the doorway, running his fingers through his brown hair.

"What's up?" he asked.

"What are you doing here?" Shama said.

"I met Gleer in the rotunda," Kardo said. "She was in a panic. She sent me to find you. She's afraid you're going to get kicked out for ignoring Dean Perbile and for messing with school equipment."

Shama laughed. "I've never met anybody like her."

"Even for Chronos, she's beyond-beyond obedient," Kardo agreed.

"Do you ever watch *UpCity Lives*?" Shama asked.

"No," Kardo said.

"It's the whole cast," Shama said. "See if you can make the lesson start. PLEAZZZZZ," she said, imitating Pleez when he called an investor on the phone and asked for more money for the UpCities.

Kardo joined her at the wall and began studying the buttons. He pushed one in the corner of the box that Shama hadn't even noticed.

"PROGRAM LOADING," a voice said.

"You did it!" Shama smiled at him, sat down on the floor and leaned against the hard glass wall.

When Kardo wandered over to join her, Pleez and the other characters were still frozen in their original position.

"When's the show going to start?" Shama said.

"Give it a minute. We share a cloud with the DOD. Since it's heavily password protected, activation can take a while." He sat down next to her, and his knees were taller than her. His feet were boats.

"DOD?" Shama said.

"Department of Defense," Kardo said.

And Shama felt as if she had run out of things to say. For a moment, neither of them spoke.

"Peke Zorn said..." Kardo's pause stretched long.

Shama waited for him to continue.

"Tell me the truth. Are you really from Lower D.C.?" Kardo said quickly.

"Yeah," Shama said. "I'm the only cadet here from a lower city, right?"

"I don't know for sure. But I bet you are," Kardo said.

"I'm worried I might be a mistake," Shama confessed.

"Well, you must be incredibly good at something," Kardo said as if he were thinking out loud. He paused then finished, "Or else they wouldn't have chosen you."

Kardo spoke so confidentially that Shama could almost believe him. She truly couldn't think of anything she excelled at, besides getting into trouble.

She shook her head. "I guess."

"What do your parents do?"

"I never knew my father. My mother died a few years ago."

Kardo gazed at her as if she were a holojigsaw puzzle he was having trouble fitting together.

"Well, you've survived on your own. That's pretty incredible."

"An old lady helps me," Shama said, thinking about Poppers. At about this time of day Poppers drove her personal security cage to her fortified bedroom. If Poppers had managed to secure a stash of estatico gum, Shama doubted whether her landlady would even notice that she was gone.

Kardo studied her as if trying to read her expression and finally asked, "You don't like her?"

Shama shook her head. "She lets me do my laundry for free."

"So, where did you get Deenay?"

"I stole her."

"Somehow I don't think you're kidding?"

"I'm not."

"That's it! Chronos enlisted you because you're resourceful." Kardo's face broke into a grin as if he had finally worked out a complicated problem.

"Maybe, but only Lieutenant Bazel knows the real reason."

"Why him?" Kardo said.

"He sent a holomessager to bring me."

"I didn't know he was involved in recruiting. I hear he's sort of a renegade."

Renegade. She knew that word from the series *Bot Challengers.* One of the characters, Wilkiam, was a renegade robot that spat at people and had to go before a bot tribunal.

Shama found herself liking Bazel better now that she knew he had a bad reputation. She wondered whether she should go see him in the morning like he asked. Although she was curious, she didn't think she would. She'd keep his secret, all right. Poppers always said, "Lettin' the robot out of the box is a lot easier than putting it back in." But that didn't mean she had to like the man or hang out with him. Her gut told her she'd be better off if she ignored Bazel and sided with Dean Perbile.

Kardo broke into her thoughts. "I think you should be at the Academy," he said. "You're interesting."

"Your ex-girlfriend doesn't agree," Shama said.

Kardo looked down at his hands. "Actually…" he spoke slowly. "We're back together."

"Really?" Shama said. "Why?"

The tops of Kardo's ears turned red with embarrassment. "We reached a compromise."

No wonder Kardo was embarrassed. It sounded like Tres and Kardo had signed a legal agreement.

"Why aren't you with *her*, then?" Shama said.

Kardo shrugged. "She was studying, and I got restless. I'm a fast reader."

"So you read all that homework?"

"Of course. I wouldn't be here otherwise. Didn't you?" Kardo said.

Shama hung her head. "I can barely read," she confessed.

"Are you kidding me?" Kardo said.

A deep male voice sounded nearby, "In 2047."

Shama was glad to have an excuse not to answer. She turned her attention to the program.

"A group of wealthy and powerful men and women known as the GodZillionaires banded together to create a refuge in the sky from the heat and crime of the earth," the program announcer continued. "The Wrestlers, the Realizations, the Molars..." As he listed the names of the first one hundred families, holomen and women lit up in front of them.

The families who founded the UpCities, Shama thought. Deenay stirred.

You've been sleeping for too long. I miss you.

Shama reached for the bird, pulled it out of her pocket and set it on her palm.

The bird blinked fast as if to wake up.

"Deenay!" Kardo said.

The sight of the bird took Shama's breath away. A fluffy piece of sky. It was still hard for her to believe that she, Shama Katooee, had such a beautiful pet. She knew she should put Deenay back in her pocket, but her caution seemed selfish. Like a miser hiding gold.

Go!

As Deenay flapped her striped wings and flew to the ceiling, her feathers rearranged themselves into different combinations of colors. Purple against blue. Orange next to green. Red next to yellow. After one turn around, she began chirping that song again. The one that Shama couldn't quite identify.

"She's showing off," she said fondly.

"I loved my bird."

"What was its name?" Shama said.

"Harreld." Kardo looked into the distance. "My parents were strict about bed times. You know...all the scientific evidence about sleep and brain development."

"Sure," Shama lied.

"After we were supposed to be asleep," Kardo said, "my sister and I would send Harreld back and forth to each other's rooms carrying messages. One night, she flew right past my parents."

"The Rivals, the Joysticks, the Onions..." the announcer said, as more holofamilies continued to light up.

"My parents never suspected," Kardo said.

"Crunchy."

Kardo laughed.

"How did you send the messages?" Shama said.

"The instructions were on the bird's box," Kardo said.

"The box?" Shama asked. She was about to question Kardo further but the announcer interrupted, "Now, for the holofamilies' coat of arms. The twenty-three members of the Realization family had a sun; the smaller Hyacinth family, a flower..."

The classroom had gotten crowded.

Deenay flew through Cleaver Responsible's silk top hat. She popped out of Minute Hyacinth's tall high heels and landed on Wordy Wrestler's thick fur coat. She was at home in the expensive fur. She was at home anywhere. She was quite a bird.

"To finance the expensive development of the UpCities, the Godzillionaires created the reality television show *UpCity Lives* about the magic of living in the sky," the announcer said.

"You really never watched this series?" Shama asked.

"I'm familiar with the program," Kardo said, "but I was too busy studying to watch Fantasm shows."

Fantasm—*Real lives in fantastic settings!*

"We watch *UpCity* for our teleschool history class," Shama admitted.

Kardo laughed. "I never know when you're kidding."

"There you are," a loud voice interrupted. Tres stood in the open door with her hands on her hips. "I thought your bird died, Kardo."

Shama looked at Deenay, a tiny sun rising and setting above the holoscene. Just then, she appeared to have landed on Pleez's knobbed holonose. To stay still, the bird beat its wings, and the colors blinked rapidly: blue, green, purple, red.

Look at me, look at me, Deenay seemed to be saying.

Slowly, Kardo turned his downcast eyes toward Tres. He acted guilty like he would if a teacher caught him pushing the button for regular-calorie chocolate cake on FoodNOW. "Um, well I..."

Tres pointed at Deenay and turned to Shama. "That bird is yours?" Her voice was an accusation.

Come here.

Deenay flew over to Shama and landed on her out-stretched hand.

"Tres…" Kardo said.

Frowning, Tres interrupted.

"I came looking for you, and I find you with her."

"Shama and I bumped into each other," Kardo pleaded. He motioned to Tres. "We're just watching a program. Come on in."

"No, thank you," Tres said haughtily and turned to go.

"Kardo," Shama whispered. "Ask her not to tell on Deenay."

"Don't worry," Kardo promised. "I can take care of that. Tres," he called as he scrambled to stand up.

Back on the landing, a man in a Chronos uniform stood underneath a sign that said BARRACKS. BOYS was etched in the glass on one side and Girls on the other.

Shama didn't want to move. She looked up at the dome's eye, naked to the night. Thousands of yellow stars, the natural moon and the artificial one advertising 3-D CopyTrav—*The fastest way to travel!*—gazed down at her. She felt puny and alone, like she was in outer space.

I wish you could see this, Dee!

But when the bird started crawling toward the top, Shama wedged her arm against her pocket.

Didn't mean to get you excited.

The bird slid down to the bottom.

"Hello," a man walked up to her. "I'm Colonel Hurley."

Colonel Hurley had raven-colored hair, a knuckled nose, and ears that stuck out like stunted wings. "Welcome to the Academy."

"Thanks," Shama said.

Colonel Hurley pointed at the barracks. "Head on in and find your name."

The entrance to the barracks led to a passageway. No door, just three sharp turns. Shama knew better than to think she could spot the SNOOP nanotechnology that confirmed that she was permitted to enter.

The common room was the size of a lifter-bus terminal with crystal floors and walls. Like the other rooms, it held a lot of wasted space. Open doors circled the perimeter. There were more rooms than there were students, but Shama remembered hearing that the upperclassmen would arrive later. Girls tore around, heading for their rooms.

We get a room all to ourselves, don't we, Deenay?

Chirp. Chirp.

The chirps were soft, and no one was paying any attention to her.

Shama wasn't worried any of the other girls would overhear. But she reminded herself not to ask the bird another question until they were alone.

Her room was opposite the passageway. S. Katooee was printed on a nameplate on the wall.

The oval bed, set on glass posts, was covered in a fuzzy white blanket. A TEXT—TechnoElectronic Xceptional Textbook—a metallic box that recorded lectures and displayed text on a screen, sat on a stand next to the bed. She had used them at the idearoom but she had never expected to have one of her own.

Once in the room, Shama took Deenay out of her pocket.

Let's get comfortable.

Chirp. Chirp. Chirp.

Yes? Yes? Yes? Is that what you're saying?

A song began playing over the sound system. *Time Is on Our Side, Yes It Is...*

Resting on her finger, Shama's bird flapped its colorful wings, changing from purple to red to blue before her eyes.

"Lights out, Cadets," Dean Perbile's voice blared out when the song had finished. "Breakfast in eight hours. First period: assembly. Your complete schedule will be handed out there. Now all cadets should go to sleep."

The bird, mainly green now, took off. By Deenay's wide circles around the room, Shama knew that the bird approved.

A fancy room for a fancy bird.

Angela said, "How many times have you been to the World Trade Center, Victor?"

"Not as many as you," Victor said. The admiration in his voice caught Maye off guard. She turned and examined her seatmates. Angela looked like a child model with hair so straight it seemed ironed, and pouty lips.

Both have super-straight white teeth, Maye thought as she poked the gap between her two front teeth with her tongue.

As if Angela were aware of Maye's gaze, her blue eyes turned away from Victor and focused on Maye.

"How many times have you been, Maye?" Angela asked.

Maye shook her head. "Never." She sensed that Angela was about to say something like, "Victor, Maye's never been to the Twin Towers." To shut her up, Maye started to ask Angela if her father still worked in one of the towers, but the words died on her lips. Although Angela had angled her body to shield Victor from view, Maye caught a glimpse of Angela's and Victor's clasped hands.

With the wind rushing through his hair, Victor gazed out the window.

Angela sighed softly like a happy cat.

Maye stared out the window but saw nothing of the cars and buildings speeding by in a blur of dull color.

At her early foster homes, Maye had learned to stay quiet and to act invisible. She even made up a name for this mode. She called it being small. Ever since she moved in with Lynn and Dan Jawalski, she had been learning to be bigger.

But right now, she felt small, really small.

Angela's desk sat directly in front of hers. Those smiles, they had all been Angela's.

Mr. Fussman glanced in the rearview mirror. He eyed Angela and Victor sitting so close. "Angela, are you misbehaving?"

"No, sir," Angela said. She scooted on the seat until her leg pressed Maye's.

"The North Tower," Mr. Fussman said. "We're here."

Chronos Academy
UPCITY D.C.
2083
0712 HOURS

"A bowl of vitajam."

"Vitajam and toast?"

"No. Just vitajam."

"This is not a healthy breakfast. I do not recommend it," the FoodNOW's mechanical voice announced.

"Vitajam," Shama insisted.

A whole bowl of orange vitajam slid into its metallic mouth, and Shama grabbed it, as if the machine could change its mind. Shama could feel Deenay hopping around in her pocket, excited by the smell or some rhythm of the bird's own.

Settle down. And no chirping!

When Shama turned and faced the room, she saw that Dean Perbile sat alone at the long table in front with only Captain Quence and Colonel Hurley for company. Not all of the cadets had made it yet to the Mess Hall either. Shama headed to a table where Liberty sat by herself.

When Shama set her tray down, Liberty gazed admiringly at the bowl of vitajam on Shama's plate and said, "You do know how to eat."

For an answer, Shama scooped a spoon into the mound

and stuck it in her mouth—sugary, delicious. Then, she pointed at Liberty's food.

When Liberty shrugged and looked down at her plate, piled with three one- thousand-calorie donuts coated with vitamin icing and dusted with protein powder, Shama flicked a glob of vitajam into her pocket.

She felt Deenay attack it.

Liberty shrugged. "Weight training. It's my hobby." She leaned across the table. "Listen, did you really get hit by a pain beam?"

Shama nodded, her mouth too full to speak.

"I want to know more about what happens on Earth," Liberty said, taking a huge bite of a bright green donut.

"I'll trade you," Shama offered, her mouth full of jam. She slipped an ice chip into her pocket and felt a grateful Deenay hop toward the damp cold.

"Trade for what?" Liberty said.

"You answer my questions, and I'll answer yours," Shama said.

"Me first," Liberty said.

Shama shook her head. "I just answered your question."

"Huh?" Liberty said.

Shama took another bite of vitajam. The mound had already grown significantly smaller. "I told you. I got grazed by a pain beam."

Liberty reached over with her spoon and dipped it into Shama's vitajam. She popped the orange stuff into her mouth. "I've never eaten vitajam plain before. Not bad," she said. "So what do you want to know?"

"What happens to kids who don't make it here? I mean

they can't just let them go back on the street..." Shama said. She heard someone in back of her. When she turned, Deza stood there.

For the second day in a row, Deza had pulled her brown hair back in a smooth, tight ponytail. As she sat down, she said, "No one's guaranteed a spot. But if you try, there's a role for everyone. Everyone can be successful."

As Shama shook her head, she heard Deenay give a soft chirp. She covered it by moving her chair.

Shama snuck another finger full of vitajam into her pocket and spread it against the material.

Vitajam wallpaper.

"I've heard rumors," Liberty said, ignoring Deza.

"What rumors?" Shama said.

"I don't know," Liberty grinned maliciously. "Maybe they lobe you."

In addition to pain beams, some Flayheads used lobe-mizers as their weapons. Shama would rather be hit by a pain beam than a lobemizer any day.

"Wipe out your memories? You can't be serious," Deza said.

"Well, not all of them," Liberty said.

"Liberty," Deza said, her voice rising to a squeal. "Your mom. My dad. They're all Chronos. They wouldn't do that."

Deenay, these kids trust adults. They don't know about all the crazy things they do. Shama knew Easypawn would lobe her.

Dee was too happy with her vitajam to respond.

"Think about it," Liberty said, squinting at Shama. "Orientation only lasts one week. No accident. That way, they can pop the rejects with a weak dose and send'em back to their parents, with a 'I'm sorry. It didn't work out.' And no one is the wiser."

"Ridiculous." Deza dug her spoon into her orange designer eggs in a way that said, *I am absolutely sure I'm correct, and no one should bother arguing. Discussion closed.*

But Liberty held Shama's eye, and Shama nodded.

We need to be careful, Dee.

Shama heard agreement in Deenay's silence.

As Shama scrapped the bowl for the last bite of vitajam, she decided that she and Deenay would go see Bazel after all. He brought her to the Academy; he could tell her how to get out if it came to that. Her next step would be to go to the Dean's office and see if she could straighten out her records. The Academy could be a real opportunity for her and her bird.

Gleer arrived, her face scrubbed, her smile wide, her green eyes hopeful. "I heard that the first period they're going to test our memory and writing skills."

"I'm ready," Deza said, grimly.

Shama knew that she would flunk the quiz in Time Fundamentalism on the four chapters that she hadn't bothered to read. In fact, she wondered if she could answer a single question correctly.

"Does anyone know where Lieutenant Bazel's classroom is?" Shama asked.

"Why?" Deza said.

Shama shrugged. "More questions about my records," she lied.

"I passed it last night when I was exploring the Zone," Deza said. "It's on the right side of Spoke 17."

• • •

Spoke 17 was to the Academy what Flade Street was to Lower D.C., *not its best real estate*, Shama thought. But at least the hallway was empty. So she headed toward the classroom with Deenay on her shoulder. Frost glazed the walls. Shama could feel her clothes breathing to warm her, but a layer of hot air wasn't nearly enough.

Time Design was etched into the greenish glass over an open door.

Before entering, she gazed sideways into the room. It was bare except for some white Puzz-covered Flairs— *Flying Chairs*—and a few photos hanging on the wall. The photos were covers from a retromagazine she had never heard of: *Time Keeper.*

One photograph of Bazel as a boy caught her eye. He stood on a stage in the auditorium, surrounded by adults who towered over him. The caption read, "Alfonso Bazel, a housekeeper's son, becomes star student at elite Academy."

That's never going to happen to me.

When Shama entered the classroom, she found Bazel sitting in the front, hunched over his communicator. Bazel looked up and smiled. "Shama."

"I'm glad none of the kids heard you call me by my first name," Shama said.

As she approached slowly, her uncertainty grew with every step. His eyes were bright and his curly hair stood on end as if he had stuck his finger in a laser lightbulb. There were crumbs on the front of his uniform from his breakfast.

He looks more like a Flayhead or a botbum than a renegade.

"I'm sorry." Bazel shook his messy hair. "I feel like I know you." He pointed at an empty stool.

It was confusing. At least Bazel seemed to think she belonged here.

"So what did you want to show me?" Shama asked as she sat down.

"Not what, who," Bazel said. "Her name is Maye Jones. She was born in 1989, about eighty years before you," Bazel said.

Help a girl who was born over eighty years ago? He's crazy!

Chirp. Chirp.

I don't need your advice on this.

Shama started to tell Bazel no again, a firm no-non-sense no, a Mrs. Poppers no, but he held up his hand and said, "Wait. First, I have something to show you," he said. "My program is brilliant. Brilliant if I do say so myself."

Somehow, Shama was sure if he didn't say so himself, no one else would.

"Program? What are you talking about?"

"A holoprogram." Then, too quickly to give her time to object, Bazel said, "Stand where those footprints are." He pointed at two black outlines on the glass floor.

Shama stared at the footprints, so deeply black that they gleamed. "You're not sending me back in time now, are you?"

"No. You'll stay in this room. Just go stand there."

Unconvinced, Shama said, "So what is this?"

"It's a revolving door, made of holoscenes from Maye's life," Bazel said. "When you're ready to start, step forward, and you'll enter the first scene." He settled back on his stool and hunched over his communicator. "Oh," he said, looking up. "In some cases, I haven't added the olfactory mode yet."

"Do I care?" Shama snapped.

Bazel stared solemnly into her eyes. "I'll answer your questions after you finish this program." He paused. "I promise."

Shama didn't move. "Tell me one thing. Why is Dean Perbile bothering me? About my records?" she asked.

Bazel frowned. "I thought I had done a good job on your records." He paused. "But Dean Perbile's so thorough. I should have done more. Let's just say—I cut a few corners to bring you here." Although his face stayed serious, he winked at her. *Cut a few corners?* So she and Deenay didn't belong here after all.

"Ready?" Bazel said.

It looks like we've got no choice but to cooperate with Bazel, Dee. With a sinking heart, Shama walked over and positioned herself on the footprints.

You ready?

Chirp. Chirp.

"You're fine missing Assembly," Bazel called out. "Dean Perbile doesn't check roll, but in Time Crimes, Colonel Hurley will notice your absence. To finish the program in a less than an hour, you'll need to keep moving." He paused. "Got that?"

As Shama nodded, she caught a glimpse of Bazel pushing a button on his communicator, and immediately a brilliant cyclone of light swirled down from the hololaser projector and surrounded her. Shama felt as if a giant had just wrapped her in an airy blue-gray cloak.

The color darkened and thickened into smoke.

Already, Shama felt as if she were trapped in a small space. "I don't know if I want to do this," she said.

"Just give it a chance," Bazel said. "It's important. Take a step forward."

When Shama obeyed, it was as if she peered through a crack in a door into a smoky bedroom. But the smoke smelled like the Zone, like nothing at all.

A person with long black hair lay on a mussed-up bed, sleeping. Next to the bed were some empty bottles, a crowded bureau, an open drawer, clothes spread around in piles. On the other side of the room, a doorway opened into a dark hallway.

Despite the cold room, she suddenly felt hot. Beads of sweat broke out and rolled down her forehead.

She wanted to jump into the bedroom and help the figure lying on the bed. *It's only a hologram!*

Shama heard a tiny cry.

The doorway framed a human shape wearing a black coat with yellow stripes, and boots as thick as Tramposhoes: *Jump Higher than the Tallest House.* A helmet and a gas mask. Something about the line of the face underneath the mask, the curve of the shoulders, the hips, suggested a woman.

"Hey, Carl, I think someone's in here," the woman called to her partner.

A thin line of fire sliced the wooden floor and headed toward the bureau. The firefighter stepped inside, an alien trudging through the smoke. When she reached the bureau, she bent down and picked up a fiery package.

A baby's howl pierced Shama's ears.

The firefighter tore the blanket away from the figure—a woman, passed out on the bed—and rolled the child in it.

"The roof is falling. Get out!" a man shouted.

Carrying the child, the firefighter rushed to the door. She passed through, and a burning beam fell, blocking the way back inside.

Flames bloomed.

"Help!" Shama cried out.

Deenay flew out of her pocket and into Shama's face.

I'm O.K.

She tapped her shoulder, and Deenay landed there.

Close your eyes if anything else bad happens.

Dee gripped her claws into Shama's shoulder as if to say, *I'm with you.*

"All you have to do is step forward, Shama." Bazel's voice cut through the scene, and she noticed for the first time the sharp white lines on the floor. So that's what Bazel had meant by a "revolving door." Slices of holoscenes from a life pied a central point.

Shama stepped forward and found herself in a hospital room. A tiny baby, wrapped in a pink blanket, lay in a slatted crib. White gauze covered her ear. Side by side, a nurse and a woman stood guard over her.

"You're the firefighter who saved her, right?" the nurse said.

The firefighter nodded. She was shorter than the nurse but broad-shouldered. A calm, quiet face, loosely framed by brown hair. Her back angled, her fists loose, her legs trunked, she held herself as if carrying invisible equipment.

"Her ear's been badly burned, but otherwise, she's okay. Such a sweet baby," the nurse said. She had the quiet confidence of a mother.

"Holding her in my arms I felt…" the firefighter began.

The nurse looked up at her. "You don't have children?"

The firefighter shook her head. "We can't."

Shama felt tears clog her throat as the firefighter leaned over and gently touched the injured baby in the crib.

Deenay jumped from her shoulder onto Shama's head and started thrashing around.

"Step forward, Shama." Bazel's impatience seemed to come from far away.

Shama had totally forgotten about Bazel, Chronos… even Deenay, who seemed to have made a nest in Shama's hair.

The firefighter looked up and met the nurse's eyes. "Take good care of her."

Shama moaned, but then she stepped forward again. Deenay gave an answering chirp that sounded sad, so sad, as Shama crossed the next white line.

You know just how I feel, don't you, bird?

A row of beds marched along the wall toward a narrow window with a view of a dark parking lot. A circle of light bobbed up and down in front of its owner, a woman. She aimed the yellowish beam at one of the beds.

Maye might be four or five, Shama thought. Her hair was mussed, revealing her ear, a misshapen mushroom, melted in a bad fire. Her eyes blinked in the light. On a table next to her was a Styrofoam jug. "Maye Jones, why aren't you asleep?"

Maye shielded her eyes with her hands. "I'm sorry, Miss Alice."

Miss Alice, just a blur in the darkness, redirected the flashlight over Maye's head. "I know you're excited that we've got a family coming tomorrow."

Maye, now half erased, stayed still. Her eyes focused upward, fixed on her dream.

"Listen, I'm not being mean," Miss Alice says, "but the people who come here, they want babies, not grown kids. You might pick up a foster care situation. But not a real family. There's no sense in you being excited. Now go to sleep."

As Shama stepped forward, she reached up to stroke Deenay. Maye had no one. Not even a bird.

Maye, maybe seven or eight, opened a door and strode into a bedroom. Shama noticed that Maye had brushed her hair to cover her ear. She wore a blue skirt, a white shirt and held a battered suitcase.

An older girl lay on one of the beds. A black cap covered her head and a thick silver chain hung around her neck. She turned her attention away from a black and silver box with antennae on the floor next to her, some kind of primitive musicmachine, and glanced at Maye.

Maye mustered a smile.

"Not another one," the girl muttered.

"What?" Maye said.

The girl sat up, and Shama saw that she was pregnant.

"Just because they take more kids, they don't buy more food," the girl said.

Maye waited there holding onto her battered suitcase.

"Your first foster home?"

Maye nodded.

"Don't go looking at me with gooey eyes like we're sisters or something. I'm nothing to you, and you're less than nothing to me, all right?"

As Maye set her suitcase on the bed, Shama wanted to go over and yell in the pregnant girl's face.

It's just holograms. Don't get upset.

Chirp. Chirp.

"That's Laura's," the girl said.

"Where do I sleep?" Maye asked.

"The last one slept on the floor."

"What happened to her?"

The girl shrugged and scooted onto her back. She stared at a poster on the ceiling. The man had dark skin and a diamond in his ear. 2Pac, the poster said, and in red at the bottom: all eyez on me.

The pregnant girl might just be a hologram, but Shama knew she'd beat her up if she stayed in this scene even a second longer.

Shama stepped forward again. The music stopped, and Maye was alone in an alley. The brick building behind her had a window open. Next to Maye, a metal box overflowed with trash.

Of course they didn't have g-pipes back then.

Maye held a piece of brown chalk and drew on a section of uneven cement.

At first, Shama thought that Maye was going to be a

terrible artist like herself, but when Maye drew a pointed mouth and a body, Shama saw that Maye was drawing a bird—not bad, considering the rotten concrete.

Maye held the green, red and purple chalk in her fist and using them as one piece, she filled in the interior. It wasn't until she colored the topknot green that Shama realized she was drawing a BriZance.

How can that be?

Chirp. Chirp. Chirp.

Shama heard banging, hollering and singing.

Maye dropped the chalk and looked around wildly.

Shama saw the figure of a man at the end of the alley.

Maye saw him, too, and climbed through the window and landed in a small bedroom with two twin beds, a desk and a chest. Maye opened another door, a closet. Two or three girls' dresses hung alongside a woman's coat, shirts, jackets, rain gear. She stepped inside and closed the door behind her so softly that it didn't even make a click.

It was dark, and Shama could barely make out what was going on. Maye pushed aside work boots, tennis shoes, rain boots, and crouched into the smallest ball in the corner. She pressed her nose to her knees.

The man stuck his head into the window. The halves of his face weren't screwed together right—the top part off center, bottom jaw sideways of his upper teeth. "Come on out, stupid. I saw you try to get away from me. Where are you?"

Shama heard Maye's sharp intake of breath. A few minutes passed while Maye stayed still, so still.

The man stepped through the window into the bedroom. "Think you're so smart." From the desk, he picked up a trophy—a girl holding a globe—and threw it onto the floor. One of the statue's gold arms broke off and skittled across the floor.

"Think you can tell your teacher some lies about me and then hide from me. Think you're better than Bill Gibson."

Shama could hear Maye's ragged breathing but she didn't know if Bill Gibson could.

Bill Gibson got a lopsided smile on his face as he whirled around toward the closet.

"Stop," Shama shouted.

Chirp. Chirp. Chirp. Chirp. Chirp.

A vibration hummed. Shama recognized the sound of a call coming in on a communicator, and she remembered that she lived in a different century than the girl.

We don't have to watch this.

She felt Deenay nestle down into the roots of her hair.

Shama took a half-step backward, and the space she found herself in was gray. She was on the brink of the next scene, and the light was full of shadows, holograms not quite realized. If she moved forward, she could find out what happened to Maye. But she was afraid, and for just a few moments she chose to remain suspended like a drop of water. She could hear Bazel talking on his communicator.

"I'm counseling a student from outside the Zone. A bit of a crisis," Bazel said, his voice crisp, authoritative.

"No, sir." Bazel paused. When he continued, he sounded less certain, not exactly like a small boy who had been scolded, but close. "Yes, sir. I'll wrap it up and be in your office in twenty minutes."

Suddenly, Shama was afraid that Bazel was going to shut down the revolving door.

We need to find out what happens to Maye.

Chirp. Chirp.

Shama was almost certain this meant: *Yes. Yes.*

As Shama took another step, she found herself looking into a kitchen. Many cooking machines lined the wall instead of one handy FoodNOW.

A small fire blazed underneath a pot on the counter—it was a stove. The man who tended it had a grooved face. Shama had seen wrinkled faces before, but the man's wrinkles were deeper and less attractive than the Trusted Wise Man Design, used by young bankers to make themselves look older.

The man picked up a tin and shook it. A brown cloud puffed out; some made its way into the pan on the stove.

Old-fashioned cooking was messy.

The man spooned some of the mixture from the pan into a bowl. Ancient food was gray and mushy looking, and not crunchy like chips or colorful like the meals served by FoodNOW.

When the man set the bowl in front of Maye on a yellow place mat, he put his hand on Maye's shoulder.

Shama's heart leapt into her throat. At last, the girl had found a home.

But when Maye mumbled, "Ouch," the man jerked his hand away as if he'd been burned.

Oblivious, Maye just picked up her spoon and began eating.

The man's eyes grew sad as he turned away from Maye and trudged over to a thin rectangular object lying on the counter. Shama remembered from some old-fashioned flat movies, a briefcase.

"Are you excited about the field trip?" the man asked.

"Yes," Maye said, reaching to touch the bright pink purse that lay on the table next to her.

"What's a field trip?" Shama called to Bazel.

"Ah, I'm glad that you've reached that point. It's a school trip," Bazel said. "Unfortunately, we've got to cut our session short. I need to go in a few minutes."

"It's good that you're awake early," the man said.

Above the label George Robertson Insurance Agency on the briefcase was a name: Dan Jawalski. "I'm taking a client to breakfast." He started piling papers inside. "Unless you need anything, I've got to go to work."

Maye shook her head.

"We're here for you if you ever want to talk," Dan said, gazing back at her.

As the scene disappeared, Shama heard Maye's last words, "What about?"

Shama blinked to regain her vision. She was standing in Bazel's classroom again. She reached up and pulled Deenay from her hair, now hopelessly messed up and tangled.

That was hard.

Deenay just snuggled into her palm and sat still.

When Shama turned to Bazel, she saw he was looking at her intently, as if he expected something. Shama felt completely drained by what she had seen. She wanted to shoot Mr. Gibson, to throw a pillow at Miss Alice, and to shout at that pregnant teenager. She was glad that Maye seemed to have found a home but given the way Maye had acted with Dan, Shama worried that Maye was going to blow her chance.

"Maye's field trip is to the Twin Towers," Bazel said.

"The Twin Towers?" Shama repeated. That name tickled her brain.

"Does that mean anything to you?" Bazel asked in a way that said it should.

"No," Shama said, feeling stupid. Twin Towers.

"Modern historians claim that the Twin Towers disaster was the event that triggered the split between the Upper and Lower Worlds," Bazel said.

"Oh, yeah," Shama said. General Mungo mentioned it in his lecture.

"Maye will be in a restaurant on the top of the North Tower, when a plane hits," Bazel said.

A plane? From holomovies, Shama knew what they looked like.

"No one above the ninety-first floor survived," Bazel said.

Shama sighed. The fire that killed Maye's mother. That pregnant teenager. Mr. Gibson. Now the Twin Towers. Maye had even worse luck than Shama did.

"I want you to go back to September 11th, 2001 and save Maye," Bazel said eagerly. "I want you to convince her to go down below the ninety-first floor. You can give her a chance to survive. Will you do it?"

Chirp. Chirp. Chirp.

Shama pictured Maye's melted ear. She remembered the bird the girl drew on the concrete. Its green topknot.

"Yes," Shama said to Bazel, surprising herself. "Yes."

NEW YORK CITY
SEPTEMBER 11, 2001
7:43 A.M.

Angela reached over Maye and yanked the handle.

"Close the door, Angela," Mr. Fussman said. His beret was drawn low over his forehead, and he gripped the steering wheel as if he were driving a race car—not a parked four-door sedan.

"We can wait for my father in the lobby," Angela said. "I know the way. I could even take the kids to his office."

"I said, close the door," Mr. Fussman repeated.

Angela mouthed to Maye, *Mr. Fussy Man.*

Maye nodded silently.

Three Japanese girls wearing matching silk pajamas and carrying stuffed animals passed by, and Maye thought of how great it would be to have two best friends.

A man in a blue suit walked so close to the window that Victor could have reached out and touched him.

"What do you want to be when you get older?" Angela asked Victor.

"Just a businessman," Victor answered vaguely.

"I'm going to be..." Angela began.

Victor cut in. "An architect."

Angela smiled as if she thought she had already earned a college degree. "Maye?" Angela turned her blue eyes on her.

Oh, no. Maye wished they would just leave her alone.

"What are you going to be?" Angela said.

Maye said softly, "I hate that question."

Angela giggled. "Maybe's funny today."

Chronos Academy
UPCITY D.C.
2083
1056 HOURS

Ahead of Shama, a stream of students entered a classroom.
In the crowd, she noticed Kardo and Tres holding hands.
Tres was smiling.

"So what's next?" Shama asked when she caught up
with Deza. Bazel had been right. No one had mentioned
Shama's absence from last period. But since Dean Perbile
had announced the schedule during Assembly, she had no
idea what to expect.

"Time Games," Deza said, pointing to the sign etched
in glass above the door. "It's to gauge our knowledge of history. They'll probably make us play Guess that Date…"

"Guess that Date?" Shama interrupted. "There's a teleschool program with that name. I've watched it for…" She
tried to count the seasons. "The last four years."

"We played it at our school, too," Deza said.

Shama shrugged. "I'm bad at it."

As they entered the classroom, Shama heard a chirp.
Luckily with the sound of so many footsteps, she didn't
think anyone noticed.

Shhh! You have to be quiet now.

Chirp. Chirp.

I mean it.

Shama felt Deenay snuggle against the side of her pocket. But she didn't sense her bird was sleepy. *Bazel's already convinced me to avoid the Dean. I don't need more trouble.*

A plain gray screen hung in front. Two walls, clear glass, provided a view into a hallway and another classroom. The third wall was completely covered by a moving collage of brightly colored holoimages: the Great Wall of China, the Nile, the Beatles, Versailles, the deaf alphabet, Pompeii, Wolfgang Amadeus Mozart and the Dead Sea Scrolls. Shama recognized some from teleschool lessons, but couldn't name any of them without reading the labels. She figured she wasn't going to like this game much.

Shama settled into the seat next to Deza. When Tres and Kardo sat in front of them, Tres twisted her neck and looked back at Deza. "You ready for me to beat you, Deza?"

"No way," Deza said.

"You're the science whiz," Tres said. "But I'm the ace in history."

They eyed each other warily, *like two wolfdogs*, Shama thought.

Tres shifted her gaze to Shama. Shama could feel Deenay moving in her pocket and on impulse she started to reach in to pet her, but she stopped herself.

Sorry, Deenay. Later.

Deenay fluttered her wings as if she wanted to fly out of Shama's pocket.

This is school.

Deenay settled down.

"Where were you during Assembly?" Tres said to Shama.

Tres *would* be the one to notice. The girl hadn't told on Deenay, not yet anyway, and Shama reminded herself to be nice.

"Not studying. That's for sure."

Tres narrowed her eyes. "What time period is your specialty?"

"What do you mean?" Shama asked.

"Deza prefers Roman history. I like late-American," Tres said.

Shama said the first thing that popped into her mind, "Everything."

"Everything?" Tres said.

"All the time periods." Shama knew the same about all of them: nothing.

Kardo turned and winked at her.

Tres smirked. "I guess we'll see about that."

"Welcome cadets," Dean Perbile said. While his Wander Eye patrolled the room, his regular eye stared straight ahead.

"Undoubtedly, all of you have enjoyed this game before. Guess that Date is best played fast without warning."

The words had barely left the Dean's mouth when a holographic scene flashed onto the screen.

"Cadets, stand to give your answer."

A rat with little nubs sticking out of its back sat in a cage. A woman wearing a white coat poked an eyedropper through the bars. From head to toe, she was a light purple. Shama knew that when Peoplecolor—*Be the color you want to be, now*—first hit the market, fashionable men and women changed colors once a month.

But Shama couldn't remember the year. She looked over at Deza and saw her dark eyes bugged out in concentration.

Tres had stuck a finger in her mouth and was biting her nail. Kardo tugged on his ear. Gleer stared fixedly into space.

These guys all want to win sooo bad!

Chirp. Chirp.

Shama glanced quickly around. No one looked her way. They were all too intent on the game.

An old-fashioned clock on the table next to the cage didn't help. It read simply, 11:57. Out the window, the propellers of a lifter and the edge of a sky city were visible.

From *UpCity Lives*, Shama knew that the first upcity was launched around 2050 so the scene had to take place after that.

Chirp. Chirp.

Shama coughed loudly. *I'm going to have to leave you in my room if you don't behave.*

That's when Shama spotted the clue that she should have noticed in the beginning. The stubs coming out of the rat's back. The sign in Fank's pet store. Rabirs for sale. Our finest rat-bird blend! Developed in 2065.

But Tres was already standing.

"Cadet Mungo," Dean Perbile nodded at Tres.

"The date is 2065," Tres said.

"Correct," Dean Perbile said. "Defend your answer. Detail the clues."

"Full-scale genetic engineering was legalized in 2065," Tres said. "The most important clues are the nubs on the specimen's back and the small B on the outside of the cage. That is Berneice, the first flying Rabir."

Gleer turned back to gaze at Tres. Her green eyes were wide. "Tres is fast," she said. "Like an RACM portal."

I was fast, too, Shama thought. *Next time...*

And if you stop distracting me.

But to be fair, she had to admit that Deenay's chirp had caused her to remember the sign in Fank's pet store.

O.K. You can help me, but chirp quietly and stay hidden.

On the wall, a scoreboard lit up with all of the cadets' names listed. Tres was the first to score. She had earned ten points.

On the screen, a holographic giraffe peeped out the door of a crowded old stadium.

Deza popped up.

"46 B.C. Julius Caesar introduced giraffes to Rome."

"Correct, Cadet Uber. Ten points."

"Who was he?" Shama asked, under her breath.

The screen filled with a volcano spewing molten lava.

Deza stood again. "Mount Vesuvius; Pompeii in 79 A.D."

She earned another ten points for her guess.

I'll get the next one, Shama promised herself, but the frame stumped everyone, not just her. It showed two old-fashioned navies fighting in sailing ships. "Ah, class," Dean Perbile said. "Go back to your history books. The Battle of Lepanto in 1571. The Muslim Ottoman Empire fought Christian powers. Penalty points." He looked down at his communicator and punched a button. On the scoreboard, each member of the class lost ten points.

So now Shama was at minus ten. She sat on the edge of her seat.

Peke pegged the year that the Chinese began construction of the Great Wall. Liberty knew not only the year but the month of a battle waged by a great African warrior named Shaka. Gleer correctly gave the date to the minute when Martin Luther King was assassinated. Shama should have guessed the date of the first game of puffer ball, but Kardo beat her.

So far, Shama hadn't earned a single point.

And except for that one hint, you've been no help at all.

Deenay turned in circles at the bottom of Shama's pocket.

I wish I could play, too. But I told you: some of us have to go to school.

Colonel Perbile glanced at his communicator. "Last round."

On the screen, five men sat at an orange table outdoors—B.C.C., Before Climate Change. In the background, a yellow arch rose over a parking lot full of old-fashioned land-based cars. The men were eating some kind of sandwiches wrapped in paper. Nearby, a little girl with her hair in pigtails slid down a yellow slide.

Kardo stood up.

"Yes, Cadet Felix," Dean Perbile said.

"2000," Kardo said. "The golden arches were the symbol for a restaurant called McDonald's, a leader in creating what they called 'fast food.' The arches used to be blue but they painted them yellow in 2000."

"The year 2000 is close. But incorrect," Dean Perbile said, looking down at his communicator.

"Burn," Kardo muttered under his breath as Perbile subtracted ten points from his total.

"Can anyone explain Cadet Felix's error?" Perbile asked.
Tres raised her hand.

Dean Perbile smiled at her, but it held no warmth.
"Cadet Mungo."

"The fact that the scene takes place at McDonald's
doesn't date it," Tres said. "McDonald's came into existence
in 1940 and didn't go out of business until the invention of
rudimentary FoodNOW technology in 2067. McDonald's
arches were always the same color: yellow. I think Cadet
Felix is confusing the yellow arches with the apron that
FoodNOW used to advertise…"

She sounds like she is reading out of a TEXT!

Next to Shama, Deza squirmed uncomfortably in her
chair. She was twenty points behind Tres.

Shama really needed to concentrate. *This is my last
chance to earn any points at all*, she thought as she waited
for the next scene. She felt Deenay's head pop out of her
pocket. She thrust the bird down.

I'm warning you.

She pressed her arm to her side to wedge the pocket
closed.

Deenay's beak continued to poke at the seam until
finally Shama just forced herself to ignore the pesky bird.

A new scene flashed on the screen, and starting in the
right hand corner, Shama reviewed every centimeter of it.
Sticking out of a bag on the ground, she spotted a box with
a picture of a man on it, wearing a diamond earring. The
word "2Pac" appeared on the right side. At the bottom, the
words in red jumped out at her: "all eyez on me."

Even though Deenay was still distracting Shama by

trying to wiggle out of her pocket, this last clue was all she needed. Bazel had said that Maye was born in 1989. Maye had been seven or eight when she met that pregnant girl who had a poster with the same man and saying on it.

Shama stood up with the answer on the tip of her tongue.

"1996," Tres shouted.

Both Dean Perbile's eyes fixed on Tres. "Correct, Cadet Mungo," he said.

"But you told us to stand, and I had the answer, too," Shama said.

Dean Perbile frowned and continued as if he hadn't heard her. "That's all we have time for today." He pushed a button on his communicator, and the scoreboard updated again.

Shama slunk down into her chair, and to make matters worse, Deenay pecked at her hip.

Ouch! Stop it.

Tres earned one hundred points, and Deza eighty-five. Kardo seventy. Gleer fifty- five. Shama was at minus ten.

Tres turned and smirked at Shama.

Cheater, Shama wanted to say, and would have if only Tres didn't know about Deenay.

You are a lot of trouble. But I won't do anything to put you at risk.

Shama tensed, ready to cough if Deenay responded, but when she felt a pinch on her hip, she knew Dee had decided to peck her instead.

You're in a bad mood.

Peck. Peck.

All right. I'll take you to the sanitizing station, and you can fly around before the next class.

Shama's promise seemed to calm the bird, and Dee huddled on the floor of the pocket.

Stroking his bristly sideburns, Dean Perbile gazed out at the class and said, "Next, you've been divided into groups for the Donovan personality test. Your score is important. Check the screen for your groups. Cadet Katooee, I expect you to be in my office at the start of Study Hall, fifth period. Class dismissed."

Inside the Time Design classroom, Shama, Kardo, Tres and Gleer followed Lieutenant Bazel down a long gray hallway, lined with doors dotted with old-fashioned knobs. The blank walls, ceiling and carpet were blurry, like the holodesigner had drawn someone else's dream. The only thing clear about the holoscene was the smell. It reminded her of the brand-new World Council building. Too clean. Too powerful.

Shama had been able to let Deenay exercise between classes, and now Dee was a limp ball in Shama's pocket.

"I imported the program. It's taking a minute to boot up," Bazel explained.

"I thought the Donovan test was written. Aren't we taking the same test as the other kids?" Tres called out to his back.

"Don't concern yourself with what the others are doing," Bazel said, without turning around.

Watching Tres' face flush with anger, Shama sensed that the girl was sorry she had traded places with Peke

Zorn in order to be in the same group as Kardo. Tres hadn't counted on being subjected to Bazel's renegade ways.

A holoman walked briskly past them, only he didn't have a face, just a blurry oval balanced on his shoulders. His body was fuzzy, too, as if at the last minute someone had decided not to erase him after all. Only the black box of his briefcase stood out against the gray.

Tres hurried after Bazel and caught up with him. "Dean Perbile said that the Donovan tests were important. We need to have the same test as the rest of the kids. Otherwise, it's not fair."

"As an operative you'll often be in confusing situations." said Bazel. "Prepare to observe and deduce, Cadet Mungo. This way." He pointed vaguely in no particular direction. But when he turned a corner at the end of the hallway, a door appeared. Unlike a modern door, this one had a knob.

Bazel twisted his wrist and the knob turned by itself, and when the door opened, he marched through without a backward glance.

First to follow, Shama stepped out into a blue sky, so high that it seemed to stretch to the heavens and so deep that it appeared bottomless like an ocean. She felt like a figure in a child's out-of-scale drawing, a minnow swallowed by a blue whale.

A few meters away from the door, Bazel glanced at his communicator while he waited for the cadets to join him.

Even knowing that they were in a classroom—and that the sky, the building, the door were all holograms—didn't calm Shama. She could feel her heart thudding inside her chest. Although the bottoms of her feet stood on solid ground, she appeared to be suspended in the air. She longed to run back to the holobuilding. At least it looked safe. Not like this endless blue sky that made Shama feel small, alone and unimportant.

Gleer stood in the open doorway, staring neither up nor down, just straight ahead. Next to her, Tres chewed on a finger while she whispered into Kardo's ear.

"Come on, Gleer," Shama called to her.

"No," Gleer said. Her lips trembled. "I can't."

Shama imagined what would have happened to her on Flade Street if she had given into the feeling, *I can't.*

"Yes, you can!" she shouted back.

Bazel motioned for them to join him. "Cadet Felix. Cadet Mungo. Cadet Rodriquez. Come here. Now."

Shama hurried over to Gleer and grabbed her hand. "It's just a holoscene," she said as she dragged Gleer out into the sky. They had advanced several paces into the blue nowhere when Shama looked back.

To her surprise, Kardo and Tres remained in the holo-doorway.

"What's wrong?" Shama called. Then she noticed Kardo's panic-stricken face. His bloodless skin. His clenched hands.

"You can do it, Kardo," Tres encouraged him.

"I'm not scared of anything...but all that blue makes me feel dizzy," Kardo said.

"Come on," Tres said. "You're going to make both of us flunk."

Tres yanked Kardo forward. Kardo let out a big sigh, and together the two of them stepped out into the void.

When the cadets surrounded Bazel, he played with his communicator. As if he thought floating in a blue sky was as ordinary as a superpox quarantine or a radiation emergency.

"Look," Gleer cried, pointing at her feet. "Oh, no," she said, before she squeezed her green eyes shut.

Shama stared down and found a city growing on the ground, which appeared to be five hundred meters or so below them. As if it were a metal forest, buildings sprang up. They were all rectangles, none of the cylinders, spirals or pyramid-shaped buildings that she was used to. She remembered that steel, which was used to build in the distant past, wasn't flexible like xiathium.

Mechanical boxes that must be automobiles scooted around on the land, rather than in the air, and Shama spotted a patch of green, a park. The trees were the color of lime chips, not the loud green of the Instant Trees that she knew. People bicycled, strolled and hurried around. No one wore privacy hoods or oxygen masks. Most startling of all, Shama saw hardly any sand.

"The scene has to be B.C.C.," Tres said. "Around the turn of the last century."

Off in the distance, the round yellow sun ruled this sky without competition. A sky, empty of advertisements—just blue. Even bluer than the Lower D.C. sky after the cloud cleansers had just finished painting over the brown clouds.

On Flade Street, Shama was used to the harsh voice of the squawker, informing and interrupting; the whoosh of lifters, hurling wind and dust; the *chug, chug* of the water factory; the breath of a mechanical giant. This street music was softer, a metallic hum punctuated by horns honking.

She concentrated, halfway expecting Deenay to chirp along with the sounds, but the bird stayed quiet.

Bazel blinked slowly at them standing together, then started walking. "You're not scared, are you?" His voice was almost taunting.

"Yes," Gleer said softly.

"No!" Shama shouted.

Bazel winked at her. "What are you waiting for then?" he said.

"Let's go," Shama called to the group.

Bazel raised his foot to take a step, and to Shama's relief, a block of brown tile slid underneath his boot. Each step produced a tile.

"A path. It's forming," Shama whispered.

"No matter what happens, stay on the path. It's part of the test," Bazel called back without looking at them. He continued walking.

Shama remembered racing across the weak beam in the roof of the old W.C. building.

If I can do that, I can do this, huh Deenay?

Silence. No answering tug. Nothing.

As Shama stepped on a brown tile, she put her hand in her pocket to stroke her bird. But Deenay didn't nuzzle her finger. The bird squatted stiffly on the floor of her pocket as if waiting.

What's wrong, bird?

Kardo groaned and put his head in his hands. "I'm so dizzy."

"You take Kardo," Shama said to Tres. "I'll get Gleer."

"Don't tell me what to do," Tres said, but as Shama

gripped Gleer's hand, she saw Tres put her arm around Kardo.

"Remember how important Orientation is," Tres told Kardo. "You've got to pull yourself together."

"It's just the classroom floor," Shama reminded Gleer. But her eyes told a different story. Her eyes told her that her life depended on balancing on a narrow path. One false move and she would fall down into an old-fashioned city. Holding Gleer's trembling hand, Shama shuffled along. She directed her gaze straight ahead. She didn't like looking at the city below. It looked so real. Realer than real.

"This path is like a tightrope," Tres whispered to Kardo, as she nibbled her fingernail.

A breeze whooshed through the room, startling Shama and pushing her off to the side. As she struggled to regain her balance, she dropped Gleer's hand.

"I'm going back," Gleer said.

"You can do this, Gleer," Shama said, but Gleer turned and ran wildly toward the office building, not bothering to stay on the pathway.

Gleer reached the building just as high winds roared through, almost knocking Shama over.

With nothing to hold on to, Shama had to crouch. She put her face in her knees, but her feet stayed planted on the brown tile walkway. She glanced over the side, and her stomach tightened in fear. If she fell off these tiny tiles, she'd be like Lesser Potato, a human projectile, landing on a sidewalk, a broken mess.

It's just a holoscene. I'm standing on the floor of the classroom.

Everything was an illusion, a trick that Bazel was playing on them.

Finally, the howling winds quieted.

Bazel balanced on the walkway a few meters ahead and twisted his neck to gaze back at them. "Sorry about that," he said. But he didn't look sorry. "I didn't intend to program such strong winds."

Shama sucked in a deep breath. She wasn't going to give him the satisfaction of knowing the winds bothered her. "We're fine!" she shouted. Then she glanced over her shoulder to find Gleer.

Kardo was on his knees, and she heard him retch. A stream of red vomit, breakfast-vitajuice, poured out of his mouth.

Tres hunched over him. They were no longer on the path, but squatting in the blue sky.

Past Kardo and Tres, Gleer stood in the open doorway of the holobuilding, her green eyes flared with fright.

"I'll be right back," Shama told Bazel. Even though the rest of the kids had ignored the test, Shama decided to stay on the path just to prove to Bazel that she could do it. When she reached Gleer, she squeezed her hand and whispered into her ear, "It's only a classroom. Just shut your eyes."

Gleer groaned.

Ignoring her, Shama began tugging on her arm.

Gleer yanked back.

"Come on," Shama said.

Gleer let out a soft breath. "O.K., Shama," she said. "I'll try."

"I know you can do it," Shama said.

Shama and Gleer passed Kardo, who still knelt on the floor. His chin was slick and wet. His skin color, no longer just pale, had gone green like an undercooked chip.

Tres goaded him. "Come on, Kardo. This is an important test. Get up, or I'm going to leave you here."

The whistle of a gale sounded, and Shama tensed, waiting for the winds to buffet her again.

"Lieutenant Bazel. Please cut off that weather program," Tres cried over the wail of the wind. "Kardo's ill."

Shama squeezed Gleer's hand. "Remember, we're on the ground," she said, but she wasn't sure Gleer could hear her.

When Gleer moaned, Shama threw her arms around her. Gleer's face, hair and uniform all smelled like mint soap.

"Why is he doing this to us?" Gleer asked.

While the winds pushed them around, Shama kept her gaze fixed on the vomit, a red cloud in the blue sky. The red cloud proved that she wasn't a skywalker, only a student in a holographic classroom.

After what seemed like a very long time, the winds finally stopped. Silence thudded in Shama's ears. Shama released Gleer, whose soft face, wet with tears, looked bloated like a sponge that needed wringing out.

Tres and Kardo huddled together a few meters away from her.

"Cadets, stay on the path and join me," Bazel said. His tone, commanding, urgent, made Shama feel like she was in the middle of a real emergency, not a pretend one.

Tres bent over Kardo. "Are you O.K.?"

"Go on," Kardo said. He sucked in a deep breath. "I think I'm going to be sick again."

Gleer scooted over to Kardo. "I'm not going to take another step. I'll stay with Kardo."

"Lieutenant, please, just give me..." But instead of finishing his sentence, Kardo gagged.

Tres stayed on the floor, staring at Kardo.

"Are you coming, Cadet Mungo?" Bazel said. "Or do I need to fail you, too?"

Tres scrambled up. "Of course, I'm coming," she said, fixing her eyes on Bazel.

"And how about you, Cadet Katooee?" Bazel said.

On Flade Street, when people didn't think you were tough, that's when the trouble began. But no way she could convince Gleer of this. So she said to the girl, "O.K. Stay here." She turned and called to Bazel, "I'm coming."

Tres had already started for the Lieutenant.

As Shama followed Tres, the brown tile pathway ahead of Bazel continued to construct itself. When he stopped walking, the three of them stood some distance from the building they had exited, the sun to their backs, in the middle of a blue nowhere.

Like a mountain being born, another office building rose up in front of them. It grew to the height of the first building. Both buildings were enormous gray rectangles. She saw a hazy version of their threesome reflected in the building's glass: a stooped man, two shorter girls, all in tan uniforms against a background of blue sky.

Shama studied the first building and then the second. They were identical. *Twins*, she thought. The queasy feeling in her stomach returned, and she felt a twinge from Deenay.

"Follow me." Bazel headed toward the newer tower, gray and proud, glittering in the sun.

Twin Towers. It was just a speck in the distance yet, but at the sight of the silver plane making its way toward them, Shama's gut twisted.

He's going to make us live through the disaster!

Then it occurred to her.

That's why you're so quiet. You know something bad is going to happen.

Even this didn't get a rise out of Deenay. The bird stayed huddled in the protection of Shama's pocket.

Tres walked a few paces ahead of her, for once not biting her nails, and Shama could tell by the girl's calm expression that Tres was happy that the winds had died. Tres had no hint of the collision of steel against steel that was going to occur.

"Tres…," Shama began.

"No talking," Bazel said. "Or I'll deduct points from both of your scores."

Tres scowled at her.

Shama glanced over her shoulder again. She found that already the plane had grown to the size of a child's toy. The collision was going to happen soon.

Pretend you don't know the plane is coming, Shama told herself and stiffened her body until it felt hard and strong like a steel building.

Bazel reached the gray tower and walked through the glass wall, with Shama and Tres following after him. Passing through holograms always created a hololight show in Shama's brain, and she had to wait for the lights to fade to see the old-fashioned office, with a desk, a filing cabinet, a potted plant. A photo of a young girl sat on the desk. The girl had metal on her teeth. Shama puzzled over this odd detail until she remembered the barbaric custom of braces.

"We're in the North Tower," Bazel said.

Don't look out the window, Shama reminded herself.

"On September 11th, 2001," Bazel said.

"September 11th?" Tres said. "That's the date of the disaster, isn't it?"

Bazel ignored Tres. "Flight 11 cut the ceiling of the ninety-third floor and *ripped* across the ninety-ninth floor, severely damaging all three staircases." Bazel turned to Shama. He spoke as if he were trying to nail his words into Shama, into her memory of Maye. "No one above the ninety-first floor survived."

A roar sounded.

So loud that only Shama heard Deenay's chirp.

It's O.K. It's not for real.

Shama didn't care who saw her as she put her hand in her pocket and stroked the bird's topknot.

Tres turned toward the window. When Shama heard Tres moan, she knew that Tres had seen the airplane headed for them. Shama didn't have to look to picture the airplane's wing, a thick knife, poised to slice through the steel.

Shama stared coolly back at Bazel. She was angry not only on her own behalf but for Deenay.

Bazel held up his hand to silence her. His lips were pressed together in grim determination, but she caught a gleam of excitement in his eyes. "One, two, three, four, five…" He punched a button on his communicator, decisively.

Shama said, "I don't like this."

Bazel put a finger to his mouth. Then he said, "Are you aware that you two just passed the Donovan test for personal courage?" His voice was triumphant as if she had just won the World Council All Worlds Lottery. "The Time Keeper's Code requires that anyone who uses the QuanTime must pass this test."

Shama shook her head. She glanced out the window and saw the plane halted, the lethal weapon of its wings frozen in the blue sky.

"What's going on?" a man's voice cut through the scene.

Shama withdrew her hand from her pocket but not before Deenay had nuzzled her topknot gently against Shama's finger.

It's over!

"Dad," Tres shouted.

The holoscene disappeared.

The two towers, the city below, the blue sky all vanished. They stood in an ordinary gray classroom again: blank walls and empty floor with a hololaser projector hanging from the ceiling.

A few meters away from them, Kardo had his head between his knees. Gleer stroked his hair. Nearby, vomit stained the plain gray-green floor.

Bazel straightened so violently his cap toppled off his head.

"I said..." General Mungo repeated.

Bazel interrupted, "I'm administering the interactive Donovan."

"Dad," Tres said, and she turned to glower at Bazel.

"I heard the rest of the cadets were taking a written test."

"That's enough, Cadet Mungo," the General cut her off. He met Bazel's eyes. Since Bazel stooped, they were of equal height. "Lieutenant Bazel, my instructions were to use the basic Donovan test. The interactive test is far too advanced," he said. "You know that, Lieutenant."

General Mungo frowned at Bazel, but his eyes looked more puzzled than angry.

"For this particular class, I decided to administer the interactive test first," Bazel said. "And I'll have you know that these two cadets passed it. One with flying colors…"

Although Shama could tell that Bazel was trying to keep his tone flat, his excitement came through.

Dee began to scale Shama's pocket, and she wedged her arm against her side to keep the bird from sneaking out.

Patience. A virtue Shama lacked, her mother always said.

A slight smile flickered on General Mungo's face as he glanced at his daughter. She didn't meet his gaze.

Bazel finished, "Cadet Katooee."

General Mungo turned his eyes away from his daughter and fixed them on Shama. His eyes narrowed and his mouth tightened.

"Congratulations on your achievement," General Mungo said, and glancing at his daughter added, "Both of you."

Then, facing Lieutenant Bazel, he said without expression, "I'll see you, Lieutenant, in my office immediately."

NEW YORK CITY
SEPTEMBER 11, 2001
7:51 A.M.

Mr. Fussman pointed at a burly policeman who stood out-side the building. "We're not going to be able to park here much longer."

Out the window, Maye looked at the cars driving past but saw no St. Pius vans.

"I better call my dad and tell him we're going to be late," Angela said. She took her mobile phone out of her purse.

Maye spotted Mr. Duncan hurrying toward them. He wore a gray suit the same color as the building and a white shirt. An identification badge swung from his neck. "I see your father, Angela. He's coming."

Angela flipped her phone closed and looked up. "Dad."

Mr. Duncan bent down toward Mr. Fussman's open window. "I got a call. There's been a change of plans. One of the vans stalled. The other van stopped to help it."

"So what do you want me to do, Mr. Duncan?" Mr. Fussman asked.

"Drop the kids off here," Mr. Duncan said. "I'll stay with them until the rest of the group arrives."

"Yes, sir," Mr. Fussman said.

Mr. Duncan turned his attention on the backseat. "I recognize Victor but who are you?" he said to Maye.

"Dad, you've met Maye a bunch of times." Angela paused. "Maybe Jones."

"Sure. I remember," Mr. Duncan said, not looking at her. "So." He stepped back from the window. "What are we waiting for? Let's go!"

Maye unfastened her seat belt and climbed out onto the plaza.

In Q-Travel Practicum, Captain Quence held up a TEXT and beamed at the class. None of the Command Staff had implanted faces and hers was no exception. But she did have an exaggerated feature, too ugly to be anything but natural: an upturned nose. Hair, dyed whiter than a marshmallow chip and cut in a shaggy style, topped her friendly face. She looked like the type of person who you wanted to see if you needed a loan of a few credit coins because you hadn't eaten dinner.

"Tonight for homework," Captain Quence said, "you'll read three chapters in Surveillance. We'll have a quiz tomorrow."

Shama groaned. "Three chapters?"

"I'll help you," Gleer said.

Gleer had waited to pick a seat until Shama chose hers, and then Gleer had sat next to her. Ever since the Donovan test, she had been following Shama around. Liberty sat on the other side of Gleer.

Little Deenay was sleeping peacefully in Shama's pocket.

"For the quiz, please memorize these basic rules of QuanTime operations," Captain Quence said. The screen lit up with:

1.Interaction with Natives through the screen of the QuanTime is impossible. But for the sake of caution, we don't want you to even try. Don't smile. Don't look in their eyes. And never, ever attempt to talk to them.

2.Keep your hands to yourself. Don't touch any part of the QuanTime.

3.No consumption of food and drink near the QuanTime.

Shama yawned. Surveillance was deathly dull.

"In a few days, we'll put these rules into practice," Captain Quence said.

"Lieutenant Bazel said we get to watch the dinosaurs," Peke said.

"Lieutenant Bazel is correct," Captain Quence said. "Since watching time causes subtle changes, you will only be allowed to view a period of time prior to a reset button."

"I want to watch T-Rex fight," Liberty said.

"More likely, you'll spend your time observing a herd of dinosaurs lay their eggs," Captain Quence said with a smile.

Huelgo and Liberty groaned.

"Surveilling past time is disorienting; more for some than others. In preparation, you'll train for your first QuanTime watch in these simulators." Captain Quence pointed toward the far wall at a row of xiathium boxes, half the width and length of a vertical magnetic levitator, with dial-locks that made them look like old-fashioned security safes.

Blow-up drawings of the control panel of the QuanTime filled the wall space. A daunting array of dials, switches and buttons: Temperature. Coordinates. Emergency Alarm. Communication Panels. Time Lapse Clock…

Kardo held up his hand. He sat in the row in front of Shama next to Tres. Shama was glad to see that he seemed to have fully recovered from the morning's adventures.

"What's it like?" Kardo asked when Captain Quence called on him.

Captain Quence grinned and said, "Past cadets have coined a term to describe the experience…*whipfrayed*. It's a combination of whirled and hosed, invaded and frozen-fried, squeezed, pulled and yanked."

Worry pinched the corners of Gleer's mouth.

"It sounds like the kind of ride I like," Liberty said, grinning at Shama. She sat on the other side of Gleer. "The ones at UpCity carnival that make you throw up."

"I wish I could go to UpCity carnival," Shama said. *8,000 rides. The most realistic holoworlds ever created and five complete fantasm cities.*

"I haven't been in months." In her excitement, Liberty jumped up from her seat. "I want to go first. Let me go today."

"Cadet Quence, sit down," the Captain said. She frowned at her daughter, but it wasn't a mean frown. The captain seemed so easy and nice—even when she tried she couldn't look strict.

Liberty obeyed, but she glared at her mother.

"We only have time for only one student to try out the QuanTime-sim today." Captain Quence glanced at her dataplate and then turned her attention back to the classroom. "Tradition has it that the high scorer on the Donovan test gets to go first."

As the Captain said these last words, Shama's heart thumped.

Tres jumped up from her seat. "I passed the advanced test, too."

Looking down at her dataplate, Captain Quence said, "I have the scores here. Cadet Katooee's score is the highest."

Tres sank back into her seat, muttering.

Captain Quence nodded at Shama. "Cadet Katooee."

"Crunchy," Shama said.

Everyone laughed.

As Shama stood up and started walking toward the wall, all the kids began talking.

"Crunchy?"

"That's what they say on Earth because all they eat is chips."

"Maybe the rumors are true. Maybe she was a tele-school student."

"No way."

Shama felt a flash of anger that these UpCity kids thought it impossible, beyond impossible, that a kid from a lower city would be good enough to attend the Academy. But she planned to show them.

Captain Quence opened the door to one of the simulators.

Shama peered over her shoulder into the interior. Tiny. No windows.

As she crouched down to enter and scooted inside, the ball that was Deenay started to unroll.

"Have fun." Deza waved.

"Good flade," Kardo called out.

"You're the best, Shama," Gleer said.

Captain Quence looked up from adjusting the settings on the simulator.

"Don't get fried," Huelgo Reel said.

"I'm glad pain's nuthin to you," Liberty said, grinning.

Shama barely managed to shoot the class a quick thumbs-up before Captain Quence closed the door. It was as if someone had slipped a privacy hood over her head. The darkness felt deeper than regular night, the darkness of dreams. But this blackness wasn't dead; this was alive and moving like the floor of an ancient ocean.

Waves of sensation started washing through her body. She could only remember a few of the verbs that Captain Quence had used: invaded, fried, squeezed.

She wanted to scream, but instead, she forced herself to say, "I can do this." When her lips wouldn't move, she repeated the chant over and over in her head.

It was a feeling of moving fast but staying still. Of changing but staying the same. Of being alone but becoming one with everything. Of standing upright and being turned upside down. She felt sick to her stomach, light-headed and strangely happy all at once. She wasn't trapped, she was nestled inside a padded pocket the size of the whole universe. Like Deenay must feel. That's when she remembered that the bird in her pocket was experiencing everything she did.

I can't help you. I can't even help myself.

After an eternity, Shama heard a click, then a gust of fresh air cooled her skin and light penetrated her closed eyelids. When she opened her eyes, she saw the arm of a tan shirt, a pair of blue eyes, a foot encased in a tan boot with red ribbing. She remembered…she was in a simulator on her way to becoming a Chronos special op. She crawled out and squatted in front of the box.

"What was it like?"

"Was it fun?"

"Did it hurt?"

Captain Quence held the group back.

"Give her a minute. She may not be able to talk yet."

She peered down at Shama, and Shama saw a shock of white hair and smelled a blast of a flowery perfume.

"My, what's that?" the Captain said, alarmed.

Deenay had climbed out of her pocket and raced down her leg.

Chirp. Chirp.

The bird sounded excited.

"Pets aren't allowed at the Academy," Deza said. Her bug eyes held shock and surprise. "It's in the rule book."

Shama forced her arms to reach for Deenay. Her fingers closed around the bird. She raised Deenay to her mouth and scolded her. *Bad bird.*

Chirp. Chirp.

"So Shama finally gets caught at something," Tres said. "It's about time."

"I always wanted one of those birds," Liberty said.

"A BriZance," Captain Quence said thoughtfully. "Well, since it's your own DNA, it's not exactly a pet. The Command Staff faced this question a few years ago but while they were in the process of deciding…" Her voice trailed off. She shrugged, then bent down, touched Shama's shoulder and looked into her eyes.

"Dean Perbile called and asked me to send you to his office after class anyway." She shrugged. "Something about your records. I'll communicate this issue to him, too."

Shama reached out for Deenay and stuffed the bird back in her pocket. *Enough showing off.*

Cchhhhhiiiirrrppp…a loud protest.

"Do you understand me?" Captain Quence said, gently.

Even as Shama tried to shake the wooziness out of her head, she knew that she and Deenay were deeply bound together and that she would die if she lost her.

"You can't take my bird away from me."

Shama had forgotten to guard her pocket and as if to emphasize Shama's point, Deenay flew out and landed on Shama's head.

"Calm down, Cadet Katooee," Captain Quence said. Her voice was soft and soothing.

But Shama meant it.

Shama took a bite of her third wedge of regular chocolate cake. Just yesterday she wouldn't have left even a crumb on her plate, but on her second full day of eating well, she felt so stuffed that she didn't have room for more.

Deenay slumped against the side of her pocket in a satisfied heap. During dinner, the Academy seemed like the perfect place to grow up, to raise a baby bird, to spend a whole life. If only…

"What do you think Dean Perbile is going to do about my bird?" she said.

Liberty, Deza, Peke and Gleer sat with her in the Mess Hall.

Gleer's green eyes opened wide. "I can't believe you haven't gone to see the Dean."

Shama shrugged. She couldn't tell Gleer, but Bazel's "Cut a few corners" had explained everything. Lieutenant Bazel had snuck her in, and when Perbile found out...

Liberty pushed aside her plate of zero-calorie ice cream sprinkled with protein sparkles. "Let's take a peek at the bird again."

Shama turned to see if any of the teachers were watching. Dean Perbile presided over the crowded table, flanked by Captain Quence, Colonel Pink-Branch and Colonel Hurley. The mood was serious; no one was laughing. The teachers were talking, and it looked as if Colonel Hurley and Colonel Pink-Branch were arguing. No one was watching the cadets. She was sorry to see that Bazel wasn't at dinner. She needed to ask him what to do now that Captain Quence had reported her bird to Dean Perbile.

As her gaze traveled back across the Mess Hall, she caught Kardo's eye. He and Tres sat at the next table over with a beautiful cadet named Rain Ivey.

Kardo noticed Shama looking and mouthed something to her. "We need to talk."

For an answer, Shama lifted her eyebrow.

"What are you waiting for, Shama?" Liberty said.

"I better not," Shama said, just to play it safe.

"Oh, come on," Liberty persisted. "The teachers are busy tonight, and you're already burnt."

True, thought Shama. Besides, she wanted to show Deenay off. She took her bird out of her pocket and set it on the table.

Deenay hopped to Shama's plate, and every eye at the table fixed on the BriZance.

As Deenay pecked the plate, the back of her neck changed colors from red to purple to orange.

Just watching me eat cake crumbs is a show, Deenay seemed to say.

Shama bent down and looked into the bird's eyes. "Chirp. Chirp," she said. *Leave the bragging to me.*

"Can you talk bird-talk to her?" Gleer said.

"Dee knows what I'm saying," Shama said, eyeing the bird.

"Oh! She's so beautiful," Gleer said. She scooped up one of her vegetable pellets and dropped it in front of the bird. "Here, Deenay. Girls need to eat healthy food to grow."

"Is it a girl?" Liberty asked.

"BriZances are living machines," Deza said. "They don't have a gender."

Don't listen to her. We both know you're a girl.

Chirp.

"I hope the Dean will let you keep her," Gleer said.

"No way," Liberty said, wiping her mouth with the back of her sleeve.

"I agree," Deza said, washing her lips with a disposable sterilepad.

"But the Command Staff can't take your BriZance from you. The bird will die," Gleer said.

"Huh?" Shama said.

"I read that BriZances die if separated from the person they are bonded to," Gleer said. "Which is a real shame since the birds have short lives, anyway."

Not you, Shama thought fiercely. *You're not like other BriZances.*

At this Deenay stopped strutting, turned and faced Shama.

Liberty snorted. "So? The Command Staff won't care if a bird dies."

The bird's orange eyes flared.

Don't worry. I won't let anything happen to you.

Deenay closed one eyelid and lifted it again.

A bird wink.

Shama winked back.

"Ahh," Gleer said. "That's so cute."

The sound system crackled. Dean Perbile stood in the middle of the stage. Behind him, the other twenty or so teachers paused and looked in the Dean's direction. "I need to announce a change of schedule. Instead of Time Design with Lieutenant Bazel, tomorrow you'll spend an extra hour at Time Fitness, with Colonel Hurley."

"Good. One less test," Peke said.

"I wonder what happened to Lieutenant Bazel?" Deza said.

"My mother told me that he and General Mungo have been arguing," Liberty said.

Remembering the morning's confrontation between Bazel and General Mungo, Shama feared that Bazel was gone and her time was running out. She felt all alone.

Just then, Deenay flew onto Shama's shoulder.

Not all alone!

She reached for her bird and slipped Deenay into her pocket.

World Trade Center, North Tower
NEW YORK CITY
SEPTEMBER 11, 2001
8:11 A.M.

In the sky lobby leading to the Windows on the World restaurant, the air felt cold, and Maye wished she had brought her sweater. Along with the others, she followed Mr. Duncan.

"He'll get us a place near the window," Angela said to Victor. "Just watch."

Mr. Duncan joined a line of people standing in front of the receptionist.

A sun rose from a blue background on the wooden sign for the restaurant.

Maye moved to the restaurant's entrance and peered inside. All the walls were made out of glass. *It's like a glass tree house.* And for no reason, she thought about climbing the oak tree in the Jawalskis' backyard. How peaceful she had felt.

I wish I were there now.

Chronos Academy
UPCITY D.C.
2083
2146 HOURS

In the communal sanitizing station, Shama sat while the busy mechanized stylist watered her scalp. She wasn't looking forward to brushing her hair out. Even the super conditioners that she had found in the cleanroom's cubbies couldn't untangle her long, thick mop of hair, after a thorough Hair Hat had finished digging into her roots.

Happy to be out of her pocket prison, Deenay played peacefully in Shama's lap, folding and unfolding her feathers like a hand of colorful cards. The bird's green topknot stayed stylishly upright always.

So beautiful. So unlike me. But part of me.

Deenay was a riddle she would never unravel.

"I'm not going to let anything happen to you," Shama told the bird for the hundredth time as she stroked it and considered whether she should go see Dean Perbile. *What would happen if I just don't go*, she wondered. *How long would we have here?*

Gleer exited the bath stall, and Shama smelled fresh grass wafting from the Back-to-Nature Toilets—*Feel like you're in the country.*

Gleer stood in front of Shama with her hands on her

hips. Like Shama, she was dressed in a long tan T-shirt, regulation Chronos nightwear.

Gleer bragged that she got ten hours of sleep every night. Now Shama knew that her own lack of sleep wasn't the reason that she was small. Gleer was small, too.

Although Shama could see Gleer's mouth moving, Shama couldn't hear her words because of the whoosh, whoosh of the mechanized stylist. Its cybratom-tipped knobs, twenty of them, scrubbed her head.

When Gleer kept trying to talk to her, Shama lifted the metal hat slightly and leaned forward.

"I'm sorry I said that about your BriZance dying," Gleer said.

"My bird's not like the others," Shama snapped.

Gleer's green eyes filled with concern. "Sounds like I upset you." Her smile was sweet and peaceful and so out of touch. "I just want you to know that I don't think you should worry. If you'll just go talk to Dean Perbile like he asked you to on the first day, I bet he'll let you keep Deenay."

"Please," Shama said. The girl's view of the world was warped. At a loss for words, she dropped the Hair Hat back onto her head.

Gleer touched Shama's knee and spoke again. Shama tried to read her lips but wasn't exactly sure what Gleer was saying. Maybe it was *Sleep tight*.

Gleer waved goodbye and ran off to bed.

As the door shut behind Gleer, Shama felt a little guilty for the way she had treated her. But she had so much to think about. If only she could find Bazel and ask him for help.

What had he said? "The bird. It's the key"? And what about Maye?

Deenay flapped her wings as if she were going to fly off, but then she settled down again in Shama's lap.

Bazel had been absent at dinner, and earlier today she had witnessed his encounter with General Mungo. It was clear that General Mungo was angry that Bazel had given the interactive Donovan test. Shama wondered what General Mungo would do if he discovered that Bazel wanted to help Maye Jones.

It seemed to Shama that General Mungo and Dean Perbile used fancy words like "Constant of Suffering" to keep girls like Maye hidden from view. They didn't want to have to confront real people's problems. It was the same reason the GodZillionaires had moved to the UpCities. The superrich wanted to forget about the heat, crime and pain of lower Earth.

Shama was sorry that it didn't look as if she were going to be able to rescue Maye. She had been thinking a lot about her, about the way the girl had knelt in that alley and drawn a BriZance as if she had owned one.

Shama looked down in her lap at Deenay, at the tufted green topknot.

What could that mean—when a girl from the past dreamed about a bird from the future?

Chirp. Chirp.

Deenay wanted her to help Maye, too.

Lost in thought, it took Shama a moment to focus on the glimmer in the air in front of her. More than a glimmer. A holomessenger no bigger than her thumb appeared about twelve centimeters from her face. It was the same one that had summoned her to the Academy. Lieutenant Bazel! Right down to the tiniest details like the pocks on his face, a moonscape of skin. His hollow eyes and wild stubborn hair. *Like her own,* she thought, as Hair Hat's fingers yanked her scalp.

Someone must have positioned this holomessenger exactly for her location because its lips didn't wait for identification, they were already moving.

Quickly, Shama thrust back the metal hat. Its twenty knobs of shampoo, poking only air, foamed white. "What?"

"…this message, Shama, I'm in serious trouble and so are you."

Shama touched the off button on the arm panel. But refusing to quit mid-cycle, the robotic stylist sprayed jets of warm water. "Darn machine." When she tried to slam Hair Hat down, she found that the metal hat was stuck in the upright position. She stood up abruptly to dodge the jets of water that fired and drenched her tan nightshirt.

Deenay flew off her lap. Shama could barely hear the bird shriek; the Hair Hat was making such a racket.

Anxious not to miss the message, Shama bent close to the holomessenger. The water from Hair Hat squirted around and through the holofigure's pocked face.

"You must carry out our plan," Bazel said. His voice was low, urgent, intended only for her. "Go right now to the QuanTime."

Right now?

"…will be there to help you. I cannot overestimate the danger to you…dire consequences will follow if you don't…"

Then the message jerked to an abrupt stop. Shama wondered if the interruption meant that something had happened to the real Bazel. Something bad. She had no way of knowing. In any case, the water from Hair Hat jetted harmlessly through nothing now. Holo-Bazel had disappeared.

Shama found Deenay on top of Hair Hat.

Her green topknot—drenched—fell into her eyes. As Shama patted Deenay's wet head, Shama laughed. The bird peeked at her but let Shama pick her up and set her on her shoulder. "You look pitiful," she said.

The bird looked at her in a way that said, *You do, too.*

It was true. Her own hair lay wet and tangled down her back.

Liberty walked into the bathroom, wearing a health suit—a leotard with buttons all over it, showing her weight: 168; Blood pressure: 120/75. Temperature: 98.23965... She pointed at Shama's hair and laughed. "Is that a lower-city hairdo? It's all white."

Shama touched her wet hair and felt clumps of shampoo. On her shoulder, Deenay had already started preening.

Shama was about to argue when jets of something green sprayed out from Hair Hat. The toner cycle had begun.

Shama dodged one gooey green blast.

Liberty laughed and nodded at Hair Hat. "Your wild hair broke the machine." She walked over to the mirror and stood in front of the regular panel, not the special one that the girls called the ghoul mirror. *See the radiation damage to your skin.* When she opened a drawer, she withdrew a box and pulled out a cybratom cylinder.

Although Liberty acted tough, Shama was convinced

she wasn't dangerous. Shama had even come to like her. Liberty didn't seem to be as obedient as most of the other cadets.

"Liberty?"

"Yeah?" Liberty said. She waved the device over her chest and brawny arms.

Shama wanted to ask what she was doing, but she couldn't let herself get distracted. Bazel had said, "Right now." She needed to hurry. "How do I sneak out?"

Chirp. Chirp.

Not now, Shama thought impatiently.

Liberty grinned at her own image in the mirror.

Shama looked at the device's package, lying on the sink. Body Builder. Stimulates Muscle Growth, said the bright bold lettering.

"You'll forget who told you?" Liberty said.

"Yeah," Shama promised.

Liberty left the mirror and walked over to the cubbies that Shama had marveled at the first day. Stuffed with bio-degradable packages of Tooth Foam, Miracle Shine Hair conditioner, Smooth Skin, Miracle Grow Nails and other products, all of which were packaged in air-soluble packages that had been new to her.

Liberty turned around to face her. She held a product-ball, Hair Shine: *One application adds a gleam of moonlight.*

"Spray it on the walls. The ammonia mists the micro-chips. The surveillance operators can't see a thing." She smiled. "And best yet, unless they have probable cause, they can't turn on the cameras. Hair Shine makes them think the internal weather system is acting up."

"Probable cause? What are you talking about?" Shama said.

Liberty loosened her jaw and let it hang slack. "Duh!"

Shama had learned not to be offended by Liberty, and she waited for her to finish.

"The Command Staff has cameras trained on every square inch of the Zone," Liberty said.

Shama remembered the signs that she had first seen in the Changing Room and later noticed over the mirror in the sanitizing station, by FoodNOW in the Mess Hall, and on the scoreboard in all the classrooms:

WARNING
ANTI-SPYING DEVICES ARE IN OPERATION AT ALL TIMES.
SPYING PROHIBITED BY COMMAND RULE 120, 453.

"But what about all those anti-spying signs?"

"Five years ago, lots of Zoneites were calling the Command Staff spies and the Zone a police state. Our dear General took command as a reformer," Liberty said. "He pledged not to turn on the cameras unless he had reason to. Probable cause." She handed Shama the Hair Shine. "If you use this on the door panels, you won't give them probable cause."

Shama slipped the pouch into the pocket of her pajamas. "But how do I open the door?"

Liberty grunted, turned back to the mirror and swept the device across her biceps again. "I thought you were talking about sneaking out of the barracks."

Shama looked in the direction of the exit. "I could just walk out of the barracks. It's not lights out yet."

"Oh," Liberty said, in the tone of someone who was late to understand. "So you want to sneak out of the Zone? That's more difficult." She stuffed the muscle-building device she had been using back in the box.

"Something tells me I don't want to know what you're up to."

Shama turned and looked at Deenay.

From intensive preening, Dee was already dry and ordered. Completely restored to her former beauty, the bird sat on top of Hair Hat like a queen surveying her kingdom.

"I'm not exactly sure what I'm doing," Shama said vaguely.

Liberty turned and looked at Shama. "The code for the indoor/outdoor portal changes daily. Your best bet is to wait for someone to exit and try to sneak out with them."

Shama nodded.

Now that you're gorgeous again, maybe I can use you as a diversion.

With this compliment, Deenay flew toward Shama as if to forgive Shama for ignoring her for so long.

I'm working on our safety.

Deenay landed on her shoulder and shuffled her wings.

Liberty shook her finger at Shama. "You owe me a bunch of answers about stuff on Earth," she said. "Like where do you buy Flay?"

"What?" Shama said, and then Liberty's words registered.

"Tomorrow," Liberty called as she started for the exit.

Oh yeah, sure. We'll see about tomorrow. Right, Deenay?

World Trade Center, North Tower
NEW YORK CITY
SEPTEMBER 11, 2001
8:13 A.M.

"Dorothy, we'd like a table by the window," Mr. Duncan said to the receptionist.

"Yes, sir, Mr. Duncan." She was an Asian woman with dark hair and quick black eyes.

Angela stiffened with pride and turned to look at Maye and Victor to make sure they had noticed. Although Victor was busy studying the display of a menu, Maye understood. The receptionist knew Angela's father's name. Everyone knew Angela's father.

Maye breathed in the smell of orange juice, coffee and bacon.

"Nothing to do but order some juice and wait," Mr. Duncan said, as a waitress holding a stack of menus started for their table.

Maye followed her through the restaurant.

The waitress stopped at a table in the corner. "Is this all right, Mr. Duncan?"

"Certainly," Mr. Duncan said.

Maye took a seat next to the window and stared at the ant-like people. The sun bounced off the glass of the skyscrapers.

"Dad," Angela said when she had gotten settled. "Maye's never been here before."

"Well," Mr. Duncan said, surveying the crowded room. "You're in an engineering marvel, Maye. Together the Twin Towers represent over 220 vertical acres." He paused. "Each floor is the size of a football field. There are 14,154 temperature levels."

"Look, Victor," Angela interrupted. She aimed her finger at a far-off stretch of brown earth. "That's Connecticut."

Maye reached out and cupped at least ten city blocks, thousands of people, and four highrises. With her hand pressed to the cold window, for the moment, she felt bigger.

The miniature Bazel holomessenger said they were in serious trouble.

Wet hair clumping her shoulders, Shama sat on her comfortable bed, staring at Deenay. She had slipped back into her tan uniform, and before lights out, she promised herself that she would escape the barracks—even though she hadn't yet come up with a plan.

Deenay ruffled her feathers and changed colors as often as Shama changed her mind about what she should do next. Bazel had told her—no, begged her—to find the time travel machine and use it to rescue Maye. But she had no idea where the QuanTime was. To get her questions answered, she needed to find Bazel but she didn't know where to look for him.

Besides, he could take care of himself. She had Deenay to protect.

Following Bazel's instructions presented so many problems that she was tempted to forget about him, Maye, the Academy, Perbile and all the rest of them. But she couldn't forget the box of confiscated toys and the expensive RACM portal at Dean Perbile's feet on the first day.

I'm not going to risk losing you. We need to escape.

She remembered Bazel saying, "Most of our traffic with the outside world takes place at night." If she waited by the exit as Liberty had suggested, she might be able to follow someone out.

But escaping the Zone had its own problems. Once outside, she had no credit chips. No way to pay for transport to Earth. The World Council probably trained surveillance cameras on every inch of the UpCity, and unless she returned to LowCity D.C. fast, she'd get caught. She'd survive Teen Jail. But what would the police do to her bird?

She heard a tapping noise. Someone was at her door.

It was Kardo with his finger to his lips.

"What are you doing here?" Shama said. Her voice came out sounding harsh and suspicious, but she was really glad to see him.

"I need to talk to you," Kardo said. "I feel like walking. Let's go to the Observation deck."

Shama remembered Bazel's urgent instructions. "Go to the QuanTime immediately." She felt sorry that she couldn't perform Bazel's experiment and help Maye. But she had to take care of herself.

Maybe escaping won't be too hard.

After she talked to Kardo, she and Deenay would go wait in the shadows by the indoor/outdoor portal.

Shama jumped off the bed.

Come.

She watched as the bird took off from the bedside table and flew over her head.

She almost ordered Deenay into her pocket but didn't

bother. Everyone knew about her BriZance, and she was already in trouble anyway.

Kardo turned to leave, and Shama followed him into the common space, which was empty. The other cadets were in their rooms with their doors closed, doing what they were supposed to do, reading the hundreds of pages assigned by Dean Perbile.

As they neared the exit, Shama pulled the ball of Hair Shine out of her pocket. "If we stay past lights out, I have us covered," she said proudly.

When he saw the blue and silver product-ball, Kardo smiled. "Who told you that trick?"

"Liberty," Shama said.

"So no one would see me enter the girls' dorm, I already took care of the panels," Kardo said. "We should be O.K."

Following Kardo, Shama turned three times through the misted panels and stepped out into the small rotunda in front of the barracks. She glanced over her shoulder. When she saw a bright ball of feathers following her, she laughed. "Deenay is really obedient as long as I tell her to do what she wants to do anyway."

Kardo looked curiously at her. "I could only program Harreld with ten voice commands, but he always did what I said."

Voice commands. Program Harreld. Shama wondered what Kardo was talking about but at that moment, Kardo disappeared inside a deep black shadow. When she squinted, she saw him again pointing at the stairs leading to the ground-floor rotunda.

With Deenay flying ahead like a flaming beacon, Shama

followed Kardo. "What do you want to talk to me about?"

"Let's wait until we get there," Kardo said.

"How far is it?" Shama asked.

"Tres and I climbed up the other day," Kardo said. "About four stories."

"I don't like Tres."

This thought just slipped out of Shama, and immediately she felt embarrassed.

"You guys got off on the wrong foot," Kardo said. "And Tres is nervous about doing well at the Academy. I think she envied you."

"*Envies*? What do you mean Tres envies *me*? I'm the one in trouble."

"Everyone knows you're from Lower D.C.," Kardo said without looking back at her. "They think everything you do is great. But Tres is the General's daughter, she feels like nothing she does is ever good enough."

They passed under the dome of the rotunda. Its center was glass and the advertisements shined through the opening illuminating the floor: *Be the color you want to be. A camera for your dreams.*

At first, all Shama could see in the circle of shadows along the perimeter of the rotunda was hallways leading to the various classrooms, but after a few seconds, in one of the rooms on the second floor, she made out lights and shadows behind the clouded glass. Lots of them. None moving. All standing or sitting still.

"What's going on?" Shama asked Kardo.

Kardo gazed upward in the direction she pointed.

"That must be the tribunal. Apparently, Bazel's in trouble."

"What for?" Shama said, looking at the figures, raven-like in their black solemnity.

"Tres didn't know," Kardo said. "Only that Bazel had committed a serious crime. A real security breach. She told me the Command Staff was interrogating him right now."

That confirmed what the holomessenger said. Bazel was in trouble and definitely out of commission. She was next.

Shama glanced down at her new boots, then up at Deenay who hovered above her.

It's time to get out of here, Deenay. I run. You fly.

Deenay dove toward the floor and then rose again toward the ceiling.

Kardo began crossing the rotunda and Shama followed, deep in thought.

Now that Shama had made her decision, she couldn't wait to exit the Zone and return home. But even if she managed to escape, how could Chronos allow her to stay on the street where she might blab about their big, important secret—the QuanTime machine? She remembered what Liberty had said. Cadets who didn't pass the Orientation testing got their memories zapped.

Although Shama knew she could never convince General Mungo of this, Chronos could trust her with their greater secret, the one Chronos didn't even know Bazel had shared with her, about the real purpose of the QuanTime—time travel. For some reason, she experienced a protective feeling when she thought of time. Sort of the way she felt about Deenay.

Kardo reached the center of the rotunda and the sight

of him distracted Shama from her problems. Lights from UpCity ads rained down on him, bathing him in their bright colors. A human BriZance.

Kardo stopped in front of Spoke 5 and pointed to a stairway. "Here it is."

Shama started climbing. The cloudy glass captured only the colors of the UpCity ads and blocked their content, so the walls simply glowed pink, green and purple. Poppers always claimed that the stairwell to heaven was steep and narrow, and that's where Shama felt like she was huffing and puffing now.

Deenay rode on Shama's shoulder, chirping away. For once, Dee didn't seem to need constant guarding. The bird was having fun.

"Why don't they have maglevs here?" Shama managed to say.

"Whenever we complained, my parents always said, 'People who live in glass houses shouldn't get flabby.'" Kardo paused to catch his breath. "I'm sure the Command Staff uses maglevs though." He started walking again. "But you'll see. The view is beautiful."

Shama laughed.

"What's funny?" Kardo said.

"We don't have beautiful views in Lower D.C.," Shama said.

When Kardo didn't answer, Shama sensed that she had made him sad. She didn't want this kid who had grown up in an invisible glass house feeling sorry for her. She stopped hiking and faced him. "We don't have nice views," she told Kardo even though she knew he'd never understand. "But we have trash wars, chip factories, thousands of flavors of gum, robotic raven messengers, old burnt-out buildings to explore. It's not boring like this place."

"I'm glad you feel that way," Kardo said.

What choice do we have, huh, Deenay?

Shama felt her anger start to rise up in her throat but she stuffed it down when she saw her beautiful bird leave her shoulder and fly above her. As she began climbing again, she decided she would have plenty of time to curse the Zone, Dean Perbile, General Mungo *after* they had escaped.

At the top of the third flight of stairs, they reached a lobby like the one in front of the barracks with two stairwells on opposite sides. One stairwell said:

OBSERVATION DECK

The other stairwell was unmarked.

"What's that?" Shama said.

"I don't know."

Deenay flew in a small circle above Shama's head, catching her attention.

Are you showing off or saying, We're running out of time?

The bird flew up the stairs to the Observation Post.

"It's just one more flight," Kardo said.

Kardo took the final staircase two steps at a time and beat her to the top.

Shama stepped through the door into a room shaped like a sliver of moon furnished with only a long bench. Since the glass was transparent here, she felt she could almost reach out and touch the skyline of Upper D.C. Signs and billboards advertised identity wands in all shapes and sizes, foot-massage socks, lawn-mower hair removers, floating beds, bicyclekayaks, jars of molecular janitors and water powder.

The artificial moon announced: *Drink Peoplecolor!— Be the color you want to be.* Each letter was a different vivid purple, green, fuchsia or yellow. Next to the brilliant artificial moon, the natural moon looked pale like a dimmed light.

Shama joined Kardo on the bench.

"I see what you mean about the view," Shama said.

"It's spectacular, isn't it?" Kardo said, gazing at the colored landscape of light.

The bright ads reminded Shama that after her escape, she'd be in Upper D.C. and she and Deenay would have to rely on their wits to find a way to Earth.

We can do it.

As if excited by the idea of leaving Shama's pocket behind once and for all, Deenay zipped right by Shama's nose. If Shama could escape from Easypawn, she could escape from the Academy. After all, General Mungo and Dean Perbile weren't used to dealing with kids like her. Experienced kids. Or birds like Deenay. Smart birds. Who didn't have to be programmed. Who already knew a bunch of stuff.

But Deenay was just a baby, and Shama needed to provide for her. At the thought of all this responsibility, she sighed. She heard Kardo do the same.

"So…?" Shama broke the silence.

Kardo just gazed at his bony hands.

"Go ahead." Shama had tried to sound like she didn't care, but her voice came out emptier than she had intended and without any spirit at all.

"Tres overheard her father talking with Dean Perbile. They're going to expel you. They said you were never supposed to be in school...to begin with."

"I knew it," Shama snapped. "They're going to lobe me and kick me out."

"Tres didn't say that!" Kardo protested.

"You're as bad as Deza," Shama muttered. "I'm not dumb. What do you think they're going to do with me, then?"

Kardo shook his head.

"Have you ever seen someone who's been lobed?" Shama said.

"Sure," Kardo said. Then he admitted, "On the tube."

Shama thought out loud, "Even with a low dose, there's not much brains left." Ziggie, the lobedster on Flade Street, was a complete simpleton.

Kardo said, "My mother works as a field lieutenant for Chronos. They wouldn't do that."

When Kardo smiled his sad smile, Shama could imagine both how proud Kardo was of his mother, and how much she counted on her son to do well here. And suddenly she wondered if *just maybe* she was being too suspicious.

"Well, I don't know what they're going to do either," Shama admitted. "But I don't think they're going to pat me on the head and say, See you later."

"Trust me," Kardo said. "Chronos won't hurt you." He looked fiercely at her. "I won't let them."

Shama felt herself grinning inside. The moment was one of those that seemed to be leading toward something entirely new. She felt sort of like she had the first time she saw Deenay: tingly, excited and a little scared.

But then Dean Perbile's voice came over the speaker. "Cadets! Lights out in five minutes."

Kardo's gray eyes lingered on her before he said, "We better go." He paused and repeated. "But trust me. You'll be O.K."

Kardo's voice, reassuring and gentle, helped her to make up her mind. He meant well, but whenever she felt herself softening, she reminded herself that trusting people had always led to nothing but trouble.

Deenay. Let's go.

Shama turned, expecting to see Deenay swooping toward her.

But the bird wasn't flying over her head. She wasn't hiding in the shadows of the corners. Shama scanned the long, narrow room, but she couldn't find her fluffy piece of sky.

"Kardo, where's Deenay?"

"I don't know. It was here a minute ago."

Without thinking about what she was doing, Shama stood and rushed to the door. "Deenay," she called as she started running down the stairs.

She heard Kardo's heavy footsteps behind her.

Getting down the narrow stairway was no problem. When she reached the sky lobby with the two staircases, she found just an empty glass space with glowing walls. Like this whole Academy, it felt cold, and the glass was hard underneath her feet.

Then she spotted a flash of color disappearing into the darkness of the unmarked stairwell.

World Trade Center, North Tower
NEW YORK CITY
SEPTEMBER 11, 2001
8:26 A.M.

"This place is really expensive," Victor said.

Maye took a sip of her orange juice. Although she expected a sweet taste, the juice was bitter.

"Think about it," Mr. Duncan said. He poured some cream into his coffee. "The suppliers have to transport all this food up over one hundred floors. It takes a lot of extra time and energy. For instance, to make this coffee—"

Angela interrupted, "Daddy loves his coffee."

"The water in the pipes flows straight uphill for over a mile." Mr. Duncan pointed at the ceiling. "So that we have light"—he took a deep breath—"and air, millions of wires had to be run. All of it has to be maintained. That's my job."

Mr. Duncan takes care of things. Like Angela. Like the building, Maye thought enviously. But not the orange juice. She pushed the glass away.

A ring tone played. Mr. Duncan slipped his cell phone out of his pocket and flipped it open.

With Mr. Duncan distracted, Angela smiled at Victor. It was a secret smile. Like the one Maye had smiled into the mirror that morning.

"We'll be in the lobby." Mr. Duncan closed the phone and looked up at the group. "They've already got the van working again. They'll meet us in twenty minutes."

Angela said quickly, "May Victor and I go down?"

"Why do you want to go down now?" Mr. Duncan said, stirring his coffee.

"We're finished with our juice," Angela said quickly.

Victor downed his glass in three big gulps.

Maye stared at her bitter orange juice and thought, *They'll go find a dark corner and leave me with Mr. Duncan.*

Mr. Duncan hesitated. "Just give me a minute to finish my coffee, and we'll all go."

"I know my way around here," Angela said. "Please."

Mr. Duncan took a sip of coffee and didn't answer.

Chronos Academy
UPCITY D.C.
2083
2258 HOURS

This stairwell was colder than any other part of the Academy, even Bazel's office. The layer of warm air expelled by Shama's uniform couldn't block the chill brought on by her damp T-shirt and the cold.

Still, the sight of the bird flying overhead gave Shama courage. Deenay's wings were the brightest red. She was going fast. Too fast.

Stop, Deenay. Wait.

"Shama," she heard Kardo call. "Are you there?"

Ignoring him, Shama raced on.

"What are you doing, Shama?" Kardo's worried voice wafted up.

"Go back. You'll get in trouble," Shama called.

Shama had something more important to worry about. Her bird. She and Kardo didn't have anything in common, after all.

Please, Deenay. Don't leave me.

No answer.

She wasn't even halfway, when Deenay shrunk to a point of brightly colored light. With her gaze fixed on the tiny ball of red, green, purple and blue—*Puff*—the bird vanished altogether.

"Deenay," she yelled. "Come back." Her voice reverberated around the empty stairwell, no longer silent but noisy with the sound of Kardo's footsteps pounding up the stairs. The thought of Kardo chasing her made her heart beat even faster.

At the top, Shama faced a dead end. The green glass wall threaded with aqua bubbles looked thick and permanent.

Deenay was nowhere in sight. But Shama was sure the bird hadn't passed her in the stairwell.

Her bird was gone. Someone must have been willing to open this door for Deenay but not for her.

"Lights out, cadets," Dean Perbile's voice came over the speaker. "Breakfast in the Mess Hall at 0700 hours tomorrow."

Shama fitted these pieces together, and suddenly the last two days made sense. Bazel had tricked her. She had never been important to him. Hadn't Bazel said, "The bird, it's the key"? Bazel only wanted the bird all along, and now, somehow Bazel had stolen Deenay and was going to use the bird for his experiment—without her.

"It's my bird!" Shama shouted as she knocked on the thick wall. Even though the glass punished her knuckles, she wanted whoever was inside to hear her.

"Shama, come back," Kardo called. She turned around, and her heart filled when she saw him approaching rapidly. But there was nothing he could do to help her.

"I want my bird. Give me back my bird."

She kicked the wall.

Hopelessly, Shama cast her eyes around the small space for anything she could use to crash through. But there was nothing. "Dee," she moaned. Immediately she felt as if Deenay were trying hard to talk to her.

Shama looked up again and found that the glass had begun shining and gleaming. When it stretched thin, a door emerged, a gray oval cut from aqua and green glass.

She could hear the heavy press of Kardo's boots on the stairs. He was almost to the top.

"Shama, what are you doing? I'll talk with my mother. She'll help you."

Shama stepped through the doorway—alone. A thin sheath formed behind her, the door closing. Through the gray film, she could barely make out the outlines of Kardo's face, his eyes wide open. She turned away from his muffled voice and found herself in a tiny cubicle, a dark holding cell like the one at Teen Jail, with a holowoman in a black uniform standing next to her. The holowoman's right arm crossed over her chest, the position favored by the famous World Council guards. She wore a black beret and thick boots, and had pain beams clipped to her belt. Shama was examining the figure's thin lips when they began moving.

"General Mungo orders Dean Perbile to report to the tribunal to give testimony in the matter involving Lieutenant Bazel," the holowoman said.

Dean Perbile—just the person who Shama didn't want to see.

"Immediately." The holowoman stamped her boot. "Immediately," she repeated. "Immediately."

Shama flinched as one of the holowoman's boots came down on her shoe. Although the holoboot was nothing but black air, watching her foot get squashed made her wince.

"Cadet Katooee, why are you here?" a voice came over a sound system.

Shama couldn't see the speaker, only the black walls of the cell, but the voice sounded vaguely familiar. Shama could almost place the speaker if only the holosoldier would stop repeating, "Immediately," in her nagging tone.

"I want my bird," Shama said.

"Cadets aren't allowed to have pets. It's been confiscated," another voice said. A pinched one, this time. It belonged to Dean Perbile.

"Please," Shama said. "I don't want to be a cadet. I'll go. Just give me my bird."

"I'll take care of the girl and her bird. You see what the General wants," the first voice said. Now Shama realized who this speaker was. Colonel Pink-Branch, Pinkie, was talking.

Shama thought about all the times she had seen Pinkie and Bazel together, in the Mess Hall, in Holodesign. She remembered overhearing Bazel say, "Some of us on the Command Staff believe." She could feel her heart pound to the beat of a new hope. *Maybe Pinkie was one of the "us,"* she thought.

"I've been thrust into the sidelines throughout this whole process, and now…"

But Shama didn't get to hear the rest of the Dean's complaints because the room grew quiet, except for the holowoman shouting, "Immediately! Immediately!"

Shama guessed that Pinkie was arguing with the Dean, but she couldn't see or hear anything. She hated being trapped inside this tiny cubicle.

Shama drew in her breath to scream louder than the holowoman, and shouted, "I want my bird!"

The front wall began to change. It stretched and thinned until gray overtook black, and then the gray collapsed into a hole, an oval door. She heard Pinkie say, "Shama, come on in. Dean Perbile left in the maglev."

Shama stepped through the new door and found Colonel Pink-Branch sitting on a stool in front of a brightly lit panel. The tuft of his dark hair stuck out even more than usual today.

Despite her worry over Deenay, when Pinkie smiled at her, she felt a tiny part of herself start to relax.

She scanned the screens lining the bottom row of an instrument panel, and on top, a complicated series of dials and switches.

In the nearby holding cell, the holosoldier kept stomping her feet and opening her mouth to say "Immediately," but Pinkie must have muted the speakers because the room was completely quiet except for an unmistakable chirp.

Shama clapped her hands in delight. "Deenay."

Deenay flew down from her perch on the hololaser projector to Shama. When she landed on Shama's head, the bird's claws needled her scalp. Before the bird could settle there, Shama reached up and cradled Deenay in her hands. She looked into the bird's face. Deenay's topknot was perfect as always.

From now on, you're sticking with me.

The bird's answering chirps sounded doubtful, so she thrust Deenay into her pocket.

In protest, Deenay's wings fluttered against the padding of the pocket. But Shama pressed her arm tightly to her side.

That's what you get for disobeying. Pocket time-out.

Pinkie motioned for her to join him in front of the instrument panel.

"I'm afraid we don't have much time, Shama."

Pinkie's eyes darted around the control room and fixed on the far wall.

When Shama looked in the direction of his gaze, she saw a cylindrical door made out of photonic crystals, the maglev and then a series of boxes that resembled old-fashioned safes.

"And no time, at all, for explanations," Pinkie said. "Events have moved faster than Lieutenant Bazel and I could have ever anticipated."

Shama wondered if she were partly responsible for the speed of the events. "Stay inconspicuous," Bazel had told her. She hadn't done such a good job of inconspicuous.

Pinkie's smile left his face. Although his expression became serious, the twinkle in his eyes remained intact. "You'll be there fifteen minutes before the first plane hits."

Pinkie wants me to go back in time!

Chirp. Chirp. Chirp.

Shama tried to think through her options. She and Deenay were about to get kicked out of the Academy. She was sure of that. She figured Perbile would try to lobe her and maybe even confiscate Dee. In a weird way, Deenay was right—traveling back in time to a disaster site might be the safest move. And then there was Maye. She remembered the girl kneeling in the alley and drawing Dee. She didn't want that girl to die.

As far as Shama could tell from that revolving door, Maye had gotten a terrible deal. Not only Maye's newfound home with Dan and her chance for happiness, but her life was at stake.

But after we get back, then what?

Shama couldn't let herself think about that. But she had to. "Wait a minute."

Pinkie's brows bumped together.

Dee tried to poke her head out of Shama's pocket, and Shama thrust her down again.

"We need to make a deal," Shama continued. "If I do this, will you help us?"

"As I said," Pinkie answered. "There is no time for long explanations—but please believe me. Bazel and I are doing everything we can to keep you safe." He clapped his hands. "Now, I must insist that you listen to my instructions. It's imperative that you go immediately."

Pinkie had broken a sweat. Beads dripped down his forehead.

Dee, are you sure want to do this?

But before Dee could answer, a deep voice blasted out from the control panel. "Control tower. This is General Mungo. Why is your viewer off? Activate the surveillance system. *Immediately.* Acknowledge!"

Pinkie looked over at the screen. It had filled with an image of General Mungo.

When his faded blue eyes seemed to fix on Shama, she felt her insides shrivel.

Pinkie must have read her thoughts, because he said to her, "Don't worry. He can't see or hear us."

Pinkie pushed a button on the panel. The screen went dark.

"They're probably looking for you," he said.

Shama nodded. She forced herself to concentrate. "Tell me again what will happen."

"When you arrive, you'll only have five minutes to recover before you need to make contact with Maye Jones." He pulled a communicator out of his pocket and handed it to her. "This will show you the amount of time you have left."

Shama pressed the communicator onto her wrist and felt the ions bond with her skin. It was a simple model with a blank screen.

"Maye needs to get below the ninety-first floor before the first plane hits. Check your communicator, but once you make contact with her, she should have around twelve or thirteen minutes to get down." He looked closely at Shama. "You need to tell her that she'll have 102 minutes to get out before the tower falls and is completely destroyed. Can you remember the ninety-first floor and 102 minutes?"

While Pinkie watched her intently, she repeated "91" and "102" several times.

"Good," Pinkie said. "Don't let Maye use a maglev. Back then they called them elevators. She *must* use the stairs."

Shama nodded. What Pinkie said made sense to her. During a disaster, she wouldn't want to be trapped inside a small space.

What am I doing?

She didn't want to experience a disaster, period.

Shama opened her pocket and looked at Dee. Her bright

orange eyes stared up at Shama. They appeared unafraid, brave.

What do you think, Deenay? Are you sure we should we do this?

Confined to Shama's pocket for so long, Deenay had stopped fluttering her wings. But now, Dee scrabbled to escape.

I'll take that for a yes. You stay with me, O.K.

Dee flew out and landed on Shama's shoulder.

"More depends on your actions than you can guess," Pinkie said.

Pinkie gestured toward the wall. "I wish you had been able to spend more time in the simulator, but it can't be helped. We need to hurry. Go ahead and step inside the QuanTime."

The maglev sizzled, and the door slid back. Dean Perbile stepped into the room.

Pinkie sucked in his breath.

"Pinkie, I contacted the Command Staff," Shama heard Dean Perbile's voice again.

"Yes?" Pinkie said calmly.

Shama angled her body to see the Dean. As she watched, the Dean's Wander Eye shot upward in protest.

"Pinkie?" And Shama turned back to see what the Dean disapproved of.

Pinkie aimed a clear cybratom container, a pain beam, at Dean Perbile.

From Flade Street, Shama recognized the changed twinkle in Pinkie's eyes. It meant menace, not laughter.

"Go," Pinkie said to Shama.

The metal QuanTime clicked and the door flung open. With Pinkie following, Shama hurried over to the wall and stepped inside.

I hope we know what we're doing, Dee.

Still pointing his pain beam at the Perbile, Colonel Pink-Branch closed the door gently. His smile was the last thing Shama saw before being surrounded by darkness.

World Trade Center, North Tower
NEW YORK CITY
SEPTEMBER 11, 2001
8:28 A.M.

Mr. Duncan chuckled. "I've been trying to reach Sol Sanders for a week."

Looking in the direction of Mr. Duncan's gaze, Maye could see a man heading toward them. Even though the space between the man and Maye had grown wavy, she could make out that Mr. Sanders wore a blue business suit. She tried blinking, but when she opened her eyes, the pinstripes on Mr. Sander's suit had bled into the air. As she watched, they grew even thicker and bolder. To shake off the now- familiar sensation, she looked down and closed her eyes. She felt someone's gaze tickle the back of her neck but she didn't turn. She felt sure that no one would be there.

"Dad," Angela said, her chair scraping. "May we go?"

"Meet me in the lobby in fifteen minutes," Mr. Duncan said without hesitation.

Maye heard Victor and Angela stand.

When Maye stayed seated, Mr. Duncan's sharp voice interrupted her thoughts. "Maye, don't you want to go, too?"

He wants to get rid of me.

With her eyes carefully fixed on the ground, Maye nodded and stood up.

"Don't be late," Mr. Duncan called after Angela.

To begin walking, Maye had to look up. To her relief, she found that the restaurant had returned to normal. She could clearly see the tables full of people, the plates of bacon and eggs, the waiters rushing around as if their lives depended on serving their orders. A woman wearing a red suit with a phone to her ear caught her eye and smiled at Maye.

Maye smiled back, for a moment envying the rich lady who looked happy, without a care in the world. She passed through the restaurant quickly, and in the elevator lobby, her clear vision still held. She spotted Angela standing next to Victor.

When Maye caught up with her schoolmates, she said, "I need to go to the restroom. I'll meet you in the main lobby."

"You heard what my father said," Angela said. "Don't be late."

"I won't," Maye said, as she watched Victor's hand curl around Angela's.

World Trade Center, North Tower
NEW YORK CITY
SEPTEMBER 11, 2001
8:30 A.M.

Shama was an ice cube bobbing in a thick, soupy darkness. Her skin was warm, but her blood and organs were frozen solid. The taste of corn filled her mouth and nose. Like she had sucked on one of the ethanol hoses that Mrs. Poppers used to power her washers and dryers. She tried swallowing to get rid of the taste but couldn't. Her mouth was dry and her breath like a dragon's, hot and fiery.

She had started to panic when her butt bumped against a hard surface.

Her clothes breathed out a layer of warm air, and she felt something stir on her hip. She slipped her hand inside her pocket and found a fluffy animal sleeping there. A bird. Her bird. Little Dee. Stroking its soft feathers, her memory jumbled back in bits and pieces. The mysterious glass building. The revolving door. A secret mission. Bazel's disappearance. The Observation Post with Kardo. The QuanTime machine. And always little Deenay. She realized she and Deenay had traveled far away, to another century. To some kind of disaster site, and she needed to move—fast. When she opened her eyes, she found herself enclosed in metal.

The box was only slightly larger than the simulator in Captain Quence's class, but the open space overhead kept her from feeling trapped. She noticed the oddity of a white roll of paper sticking out from the metal wall, but didn't try to make sense of this detail.

Are you O.K.?

The ball of fluff shivered in response.

Shama felt a flash of worry until she concentrated on standing and couldn't.

You're just taking a second to recover like me.

Although her butt pressed against a hard surface, Shama's mind floated away like a loose kite, providing a view of herself from above, the top of her own dark head. Her hair had dried into some kind of sculpture. She pressed her palms against the sides of the stall, trying to return to Earth without crashing.

From somewhere deep inside her throat, she summoned a pool of spit and swallowed to get rid of the taste of ethanol. She began panting to warm up her insides.

As Shama felt the blood start chugging through her veins, her organs—frozen meat—began melting to slush. After a few moments, when she could focus on the floor and see its plain grayness, she knew that her mind had landed.

Shama looked down and found that she was sitting on a white chair. The idearoom on Flade Street had ancient bathrooms without water sprays, air blowers, sanitizing mists, germ killers. She guessed that this chair had to be a primitive toilet.

When she felt Deenay's wings flutter, she was relieved. Her bird was fine.

Just then, Deenay began hopping around in Shama's pocket. In fact, the bird was more than fine; she was energetic.

How do you do this so easily?

But this was no time to have a conversation with Deenay.

A door to a nearby stall closed. The sound of footsteps filled her with a sense of urgency.

She had to concentrate all her energy into her right leg; she ordered it to move.

Her leg started trembling, and slowly it rose up off the floor. She turned her attention to her other leg. She slipped off the toilet and was glad when her legs supported her weight.

Go. You've got to go! she told herself.

But she felt confused. She wasn't sure if she needed to move for herself or for someone else.

As Shama tried to recall her purpose, she pictured the girl named Maye Jones. Maye was bent over the alley floor, and Shama could see the strange mushroom of her melted ear. When Mr. Gibson loomed near the entrance to the alley, Maye bolted away. Bits and pieces of colored chalk scattered around the drawing of Deenay.

Everyone deserves a break, Shama thought as she slipped out of the stall.

Stay in my pocket.

Chirp. Chirp.

And hush. This isn't a game.

Dee went quiet.

Maye—not the holographic one, the real Maye—had her back to Shama, facing the mirror, and Shama concentrated on keeping her footsteps soft and light as she headed toward her.

World Trade Center, North Tower
NEW YORK CITY
SEPTEMBER 11, 2001
8:31 A.M.

In the mirror, Maye examined her own familiar face—her light brown skin, hair that had grown frizzier since that morning and now completely hid her damaged ear.

I hate Angela. And I hate Victor...

And remembering Dan's awkward pat on her shoulder that morning,

I hate Dan.

I hate all of them!

Maye turned on the water to wash her hands, and that's when she noticed a girl—dressed all in tan—standing at the next sink over. Although she was shorter than Maye and smaller, Maye guessed that they were about the same age.

A riot of shiny black hair—shinier than any hair Maye had ever seen—exploded out of her head and encased the girl's shoulders and back in a strange hairdo, sort of a black birdcage. Her teeth were whiter than a movie star's.

But the expression on the girl's mirrored reflection made Maye's heart stop. Tears welled up in the girl's brown eyes. Her fists were clenched. The girl's total attention was fixed on Maye. The girl took a deep breath, and her expression grew calmer. "You're Maye Jones."

Maye nodded. She didn't remember ever meeting this girl. "Who are you?"

"Shama Katooee," the girl said.

Maye cocked her head. Her accent was funny. Sort of like a television announcer's but looser. "Where are you from?"

"The future."

"Huh?" Maye said. She felt her heart thump and realized that she may have stumbled into what Dan would call a "situation." *This girl could be crazy*, she told herself.

Maye didn't bother to turn off the water. If she made herself small and snuck quietly away, perhaps she could keep a bad day from growing worse and could avoid a scene with the crazy girl. She turned, intending to hurry out the door. But before she could leave, strong fingers gripped her arm.

Maye's legs tensed.

Run out the door, and don't look back.

The girl said, "I need thirty seconds."

It wasn't a plea or a command. Just a statement, but Maye found herself slowly turning around and facing the girl.

Gold flecked Shama's brown eyes, and when they locked into Maye's, Maye felt helpless to move, to breathe.

"Listen," Shama said. She spoke softly and confidentially, like she was the best friend that Maye had always longed for. "Something terrible is going to happen." She paused. "You need to leave this building."

When Shama glanced down at her wrist, Maye noticed that the watch the girl wore was weird. It had no band. Only a screen with the minutes and seconds, 12:12, displayed in black.

How did the watch stay attached to her arm?

"An airplane's going to hit—in twelve minutes," Shama said.

"What?" Maye burst out. The sound of her own voice proved that she was awake and not dreaming.

"The whole building's going to collapse," Shama said. She knocked the side of her head with her fist. "I'm sure he said in 102 minutes."

Maye's damaged ear felt hot, and panic gripped her throat.

"Listen," Shama repeated more slowly. "This is the most important part."

Shama glanced at her wrist again, and Maye noticed that the screen on the girl's odd watch now showed 11:08.

"In eleven minutes," Shama said. "You need to be below the ninety-first floor. Use a stairwell. No maglev—I mean elevator," Shama said. "Do you understand?"

Maglev?

"After the plane hits, you have 102 minutes to get to the bottom and out of the building, as far away as you can." Shama paused as if to give Maye time to absorb her warning. "Now go."

Maye said simply, "I can't. I'm with my school group."

Shama's eyes fluttered wildly. "I didn't care at first. But everything else has gone wrong, and I won't let you"— she paused—"die."

The word "die" was still reverberating off the walls when Shama swooped down. Her black hair curtained her face as she grabbed Maye's pink purse. The one that Lynn had given her for her birthday.

For an instant, too stunned to move, Maye watched as Shama scurried for the door.

When the door banged shut behind Shama, Maye recovered herself. "Wait! Give me my purse back."

Maye called out, "Thief!"

World Trade Center, North Tower
NEW YORK CITY
SEPTEMBER 11, 2001
8:33 A.M.

To get to the stairwell, Shama had to dodge a man wearing a box around his neck that he held up to his face at a group; throngs of people in awkward-looking clothes and cumbersome shoes. How did people walk in those things? She stopped underneath the red-and-white exit sign, holding the thing that Maye had called a purse.

Ionic attachment must not have been invented yet, or no way would the girl care about such a clunky hard object as this. The only thing Shama liked about the purse was its color, bright pink.

Almost as colorful as you.

Chirp. Chirp. Deenay threw herself against the walls of Shama's pocket.

Not now.

When Maye saw her, Shama lifted up the purse and waved.

Maye looked furious and determined.

Certain the girl would follow, Shama opened the door to the stairwell and stepped inside. She jammed her arm against the pocket to keep Deenay trapped.

As Shama stared down at the clean gray stairwell, cleaner than any she'd ever seen on Flade Street, she glanced at her communicator. Large numbers filled the screen: 9:20. Nine minutes and twenty seconds until the airplane hit. She jumped down the first few steps, and when her feet landed, she started running.

Deenay's claws near the opening of her pocket terrified Shama.

Stay with me.

Chirp. Chirp.

As Shama wedged Maye's purse more tightly against her side, she heard the stairwell door close. Behind her, Maye's footsteps thumped at a rapid pace, but not nearly as fast as her own. She was just passing the number on the next door, 103. The stairs stretched out before her, and she ordered herself to concentrate, to take two at a time.

She couldn't hear the airplane yet, but she could sense it. Having seen that plane's wing in holographic form, she never wanted to face the real version.

Every step I take means that you, Maye and me are farther away from that airplane. Farther away from that wing.

As Shama's feet pummeled the stairs, she sensed that Dean Perbile and General Mungo, each carrying a lobe, had joined the chase. And Easypawn, too. Because of his collapsed face, Nylon was only able to hobble slowly and painfully down these stairs. Poppers cursed each and every step. "Get me my estatico gum, lazy girl." Mr. Gibson threw beer bottles at her, and the glass splintered into thousands of pieces on the stairs.

Shama found herself running from Officer Dare at tele-school. From the impossible tests at the Academy. From the many nights she had gone to bed hungry on Flade Street.

Her feet barely touched the next landing, and she glanced at her communicator: 8:23.

As the race overtook her, Shama felt that she and Deenay were no longer alone. The holopeople in General Mungo's class who had died of accidents, war, disease had appeared. Like Pinkie's hologuard in the holding cell, she felt them flanking her.

Shama ran not only for Deenay and herself, but for all the people, young and old, who had died too early, who hadn't lived out their full lives. And for Maye Jones and every other girl and boy in the whole universe who'd gotten a burnt deal.

She ran for all the people that the UpCities liked to forget, that General Mungo and Dean Perbile wanted to ignore.

Shama gazed up toward the gray ceiling. Like the lady in the red suit in the restaurant. Like all the other innocent people in this building. Like her mother who had been just crossing the street when the lifter crashed on top of her. Like Bazel's father, who only needed one vial of vaccine.

The clatter of her feet sounded hollow in the great empty space, and it occurred to her what she was really running from. General Mungo had told her in his lecture, right before she had fallen asleep. He threw out the term proudly in the way people did who could read well and thought words were all-important. The Constant of Suffering.

Suffering was dressed up as an airplane and was chasing her. And Shama was outrunning even that.

With Deenay safe in her pocket, she was running faster than she had ever run.

She had never felt so completely happy.

World Trade Center, North Tower
NEW YORK CITY
SEPTEMBER 11, 2001
8:36 A.M.

The promise of a thief—what's that worth? Maye despaired, as she thought of her beautiful pink clutch with fifteen dollars inside and a new tube of lipstick. She concentrated so hard on the stairs that it wasn't until she saw the number 101 on the back of a door and felt her underarms moist and sticky that she asked herself, *What are you doing?*

"Give me my purse!" she shouted at Shama again.

"Just a few more floors."

Shama's voice sounded far away, and Maye felt woozy gazing down at the gray stairwell. That purse was her favorite birthday present. The first birthday present Maye had ever received. Besides, if she lost it, Maye wouldn't be able to tell Lynn and Dan the truth. That Maye had cared about the purse so much that she had chased a thief down a stairwell. Because, of course, her foster parents wouldn't believe her tale about the girl in a bathroom who claimed to be from the future.

Maye tried to calm herself. She had left Mr. Duncan and the kids less than ten minutes ago. He was still drinking his coffee. Probably Mr. Duncan hadn't even asked for the check yet. She guessed Mrs. Calabrese, her teacher and the rest of the class were still in the parking garage fooling with the broken van. And Angela and Victor—well, she didn't even want to think about them. Probably in some dark corner somewhere.

Maye was approaching the ninety-third floor. It would take only a few minutes to exit the stairwell, find an elevator and shoot down to the lobby. She had a little more time.

No one will miss me.

Maye listened to the sound of Shama running down the stairs. In the distance, she could see the number 91 written on the back of a door. The ninety-first floor. According to the girl, the magic floor. Hopefully, Shama would stop there.

But when Shama passed the ninety-first floor without slowing, Maye felt a knot in her stomach, the familiar knot of loss.

She's not going to give me back my purse.

Maye arrived at the landing for the ninetieth floor and stopped. Reaching for the door knob, she thought, *I'll find the closest elevator. I'll get to the lobby before I get into trouble.*

"Maye," she heard Shama's voice say, thinned by all the metal.

When Maye twisted over the banister and stared down into the well, she saw Shama on the landing below. The purse, a slice of pink, was pressed awkwardly against her hip pocket.

"Please. I'll give you what you want," Shama said.

Maye jogged down the stairs to reach Shama.

She was just a few steps away when Shama transferred Maye's purse to her other hand and something flew into the air from Shama's pocket.

Shama gazed upward. With her wild hair and unusual clothing, she looked like a sorceress in a book of fairy tales, not a girl from the future.

Then, following Shama's gaze, Maye spotted the bird. More beautiful than any bird she'd ever seen, more like a jigsaw of bright colors, glowing blue, green, red and purple. A fuzzy texture woven with light.

"What's that?" she demanded, between gasps for breath.

But she already knew.

It's the bird in my dreams!

Maye reached the landing and stood next to Shama. The bird circled them, flapping its rainbow-colored wings.

"She's my BriZance. The first one was made in 2...0...8...3." Shama spelled out the year as if Maye were dumb. "The future." She paused. "Her name is Deenay. Do you believe me now?"

Am I dreaming? Or crazy?

Chirp. Chirp. Chirp.

Maye could barely hear the bird's tune over a dull buzz, the sound of a thousand mosquitoes or an electrical system gone wild.

"Can you hear it?" Shama said. She pointed toward the ceiling. "One of those...airplanes is coming." And her eyes darted to her funny watch.

Now that she had stopped running, Maye realized that the background noise was getting louder.

But it could be anything. Anything is more likely than an airplane.

The brightly lit bird still flew overhead, and every flap of its glowing wings— purple, green, red, blue—proved that the bird belonged to the future.

But Maye refused to believe the rest of Shama's story. A plane wouldn't fly into the Twin Towers. Men like Mr. Duncan wouldn't let that happen. Shama was lying about that. Maye was still struggling to figure Shama out when she noticed her pink purse. "Can I just have my purse back?" she asked.

Without taking her eyes from her watch, Shama handed it to her.

Maye opened it and checked the contents: her pink Kiss lipstick, some coins, her three five-dollar bills, pen and bands for her hair. It was all there. She heard a chirp and found that the bird with the funny name had landed on the rail near where she stood. Its orange eyes studied her.

Behind the bird, she clearly saw the gray door. It had the number 89 written on it.

But now that Maye could leave, she wanted to stay.

If Shama's warning was right, Maye ought to feel afraid. Yet with the bird strutting around on the rail, chirping, she felt strangely happy.

The red, purple, blue and green bird looked so out of place, so hopeful, in the stairwell of this gray building.

Mr. Duncan.

In case Shama wasn't lying, Maye ought to at least try to warn Angela's father. He'd know what to do.

Clutching the pink purse to her chest, Maye had taken a step toward the door when she heard Shama shout, "I'm so stupid!"

Maye turned around and found Shama, still staring at

her wrist. "I was a fool. They're just going to leave us here. We're not going to get back."

Despite herself, Maye was curious. "What?" she said, but had trouble making herself heard. The background noise had swelled to a dull roar, and the stairwell had gone all shimmery.

Shama gazed up wildly at the ceiling. "I know you're there! I can feel you," she shouted.

Waves of air lapped at her so furiously that Maye felt like she was watching a broken television that could no longer be repaired. Was this what Shama was talking about?

"You're watching me," Shama said.

Before Maye could ask Shama if she were experiencing the same sensation that creeped Maye out, Shama dropped her head into her hands.

Maye took a step toward her to touch her, say something, anything to comfort her, when Shama looked up. Her dark eyes were watery but the expression on her face could only be described as fierce.

"I hate them. I hate them all," Shama mumbled.

"I know," Maye said.

Shama glanced at her watch, then quickly she looked again at Maye, her eyes narrowing. "I thought you had the worst luck but you don't. We're the same."

Maye started to ask, "What do you mean?" But to her surprise, in between the shimmers, Maye caught sight of the bird, and as if she could read its thoughts, she knew that it was flying toward her.

"Deenay?" Shama called. Her tone was full of wonderment.

By the time the bird's claws pinched Maye's skin, the air had settled down, and she could see the bird more clearly. Its feathers shone bright like it had swallowed different-colored lights. Forgetting everything else, Maye looked at Shama in awe.

Shama's mouth dropped open.

Maye smiled and steadied her lower arm.

The bird started cleaning its brilliant wings; the feathers riffled like so many different-colored cards.

Chirp. Chirp. Chirp.

It was crazy, but Maye sensed the bird was saying, "I love you. I love you both." Maye would give anything to own a bird like this.

"May I pet your bird?" Without waiting for permission, she stroked the bird's green topknot.

Shama pressed her hand to her heart. "That means..."

Maye would always remember the sight of the bird from her dreams, a bright purple now, leaving her arm and soaring to her shoulder in the second before the explosion.

A blast sounded; the lights went out; the sides of the room buckled. A gust of hot air turned the room into an oven. Maye's lungs filled with dust, smoke and the smell of gasoline.

As if through a closed door, she heard Shama's voice. "Maye, you have to make it. Because...there's me."

Because there's me?

"What?" Maye shouted.

The ceiling split and a beam crashed through.

"Look out," Maye cried. When she reached for Shama,

she grasped nothing at all, as the shape that had been Shama vanished before Maye's eyes. One minute Shama crouched in front of her, and the next she evaporated like morning dew.

Maye fell forward onto the landing. Her knees hit hard. Something knocked her back. She covered her head and curled into a small ball.

Maye smelled the smoke, and thought, *Not a fire.*

Please! Anything but a fire.

Maye remembered fire. The lines of red hot light that had raced toward her.

Fire took her mother's life, and fire burned her ear. She remembered the searing pain.

And she would never forget the ugly, black, stinky smoke that poured into her lungs although she willed it to go away.

Suddenly, she remembered an unfamiliar voice shouting, "There's a little girl."

A rough pair of hands had lifted her from that long-ago fire.

Then she thought of Shama Katooee, the girl with the wild hair from the future who had come to warn her. And the girl's beautiful bird. And even as Maye's lungs filled with smoke, she remembered what she had known and yet forgotten. What she heard every day in chapel at school. What seemed impossible to believe.

No matter what. Someone cared.

Still crouched into a ball with her eyes closed, Maye pictured the near future: the red devil of a fire that raged above her. The rubble that she would have to crawl over in the next hour. The train of people moving patiently but urgently down these stairs, and the world's greatest city shaken but proud.

And before Maye opened her eyes, she imagined Dan and Lynn's smiling faces when she ran into their arms. For just a moment, she was able to lose herself in their warm hugs.

The lights in the stairwell flickered and came on.

When Maye stood up, Shama and her bird already seemed like a crazy person's dream. Maye Jones, Maybe no longer, picked up her dirty purse and started down the stairs.

Chronos Academy
UPCITY D.C.
2083
1625 HOURS

Music!

At first, the song sounded like Flade Street on a good day. People's hushed voices: "An orphan. Just a random girl. Are you sure? Maybe's there's something unique about her...Who she is anyway..." mingled with a lifter's whirling, a Rabir's squeaks, the sizzle of chips frying. As the voices grew louder, angrier, sadder—"You have no idea what you're going to do. The chaos you'd be unleashing in the world"— the music changed into the slow drag of the water-factory workers heading toward their shift, the *shhhh* of Poppers' radiator dryer, the crackle of the broken imagetube in the idearoom, the stinging whoosh of dust and the chirps of a bird singing a familiar tune.

This time, Shama recognized the melody, the song her mother used to sing, and managed to remember a few words. Something about trees, grass and a strange word— "terangelo."

A sharp blast nearly split her eardrums. Officer Dare's whistle for teleschool. Shama opened her eyes.

The room was small, narrow, plain and too bright and too clean. Like a clinic.

Behind a clear glass panel, Bazel sat in a chair with his

legs crossed. She glanced at the sign on the wall, reading QUARANTINE in bold black letters, and understood why he sat on the other side of the glass.

As he stared intently at her, Bazel snapped his fingers, and the haunting music stopped.

"Could you turn the music back on?" Shama asked, unsure whether or not he could hear her.

But he answered immediately, "What music?" Then he asked, "How are you feeling?"

Shama noticed for the first time her throbbing head. She reached up and touched a moist bandage. "I could feel you watching me. I thought I was going to die."

Bazel smiled and shrugged. His uniform looked even messier than usual. "You'd be dead if you hadn't gone back."

Shama said, "I know." She'd never forget the sight of Deenay landing on Maye's arm. The delight on Maye's face. Shama's glimpse at that moment of Maye's melted ear.

So strange!

Shama realized that by saving someone else, she'd saved herself. But she knew without asking that she'd lost her bird. The world was different. Deenay was gone. Her eyes welled with tears.

Bazel nodded approvingly. "Maye Jones was your great-great-grandmother," he said. "How did you figure it out?"

"Deenay went to her," Shama said. "She'd never done that before."

Dee was part of me. So was Maye.

"That bandage gives you an excuse," Bazel said.

"Not now," Shama muttered. By his tone, she guessed he had hatched another scheme. And that he wanted her to be in on it. "I'm too sad." She had been a fool to let Deenay out of her pocket, but then if she hadn't, she wouldn't have known...

Her thoughts trailed off.

"Listen to me," Bazel said. "We don't have much time. I've magnetized this area. We have only a few minutes to talk when no one will hear or view us." Bazel paused. "That head injury of yours..." He paused again. "It gives you safe passage out of Chronos if you want. I felt I owed you that." He winked at her. "But you'll have to pretend you've lost your memory."

Shama felt a surge of anger. "Perbile would lobe me, wouldn't he?" she demanded.

Bazel's eyes flared open. "No." For the first time, she sensed that he did care about her. Maybe a little.

"Chronos doesn't harm children," Bazel said. His voice was reassuring. "Just a little hypnosis to make you forget the last few days." He gave a half-sad smile. "Somehow, I think you can manage to avoid even that mild fate."

Through the dull throb of her pain, Shama tried to absorb what Bazel had said. She could go back to Flade Street. She'd have to make up with Poppers. But she could win the old lady back. Then there was Easypawn and Nylon. *Harder*, she thought, but she could manage. Besides, in the time that had passed, anything could have happened. Easypawn could even be gone. And teleschool. Of course, she could catch up. But at the Academy, she had learned just how poor an education teleschool really was.

"Alternatively, General Mungo says you can stay at the Academy. It's up to you," Bazel said.

Shama could be with Kardo, Liberty, Gleer and all of the other kids who knew nothing of Flade Street and thought that life within the invisible walls of the Zone mattered. She could live in the Zone, a place without weather, smells, problems or daily excitement. She'd have all she wanted to eat. She pictured the shiny FoodNOW and the soy tacos, caturas and real chocolate cake she'd devour at every meal.

But Chronos hypnotized kids who didn't make it, and she would flunk Time Fundamentalism. This time, she'd have to return to the Academy alone, without her bird. A memory of something Bazel had said to her floated through her head: "Time is a complicated mix of nodes that can be changed—or areas of free will, if you want to call them that—and lines of predestination that man cannot affect."

"Time is a mixture of bad choices," Shama said.

Bazel gave a short grunt of a laugh.

As Shama spoke again, "I don't understand anything," the last few days flashed before her eyes: stealing Deenay, going to the Academy, trying to sneak out, rescuing Maye Jones. She decided that she had made some good decisions. But how this had happened, she had no idea. She felt as if someone or something had been behind her, nudging her in a certain direction like a mother tending a child.

That's when she noticed a shadow on the white sheet, which all the brightness of the room didn't penetrate. A small black ball. But just as she reached for it, the sun shifted; it shimmered, then vanished. As if it had never existed in the first place.

Bazel pointed his finger at her. "You've got to decide. No one else can do it for you."

Shama wished for that nudge now. "I don't know what to do," she admitted.

The wall began gleaming, and a door appeared in the anteroom where Bazel sat. Colonel Pink-Branch stepped through. His face was calm, a happy-go-lucky teacher again, not the officer who had threatened Dean Perbile with a pain beam. "Bazel, Mungo's on his way. Two more minutes." He turned and grinned at Shama as if she were a gift of ten million credit coins.

Shama remembered the tribunal convened by Mungo to investigate Bazel. "You're not in trouble anymore?"

"No, Cadet Katooee," Pinkie answered her question to Bazel. "We're not. With your help, we've ushered in a new day at Chronos."

"Disasters, wars, tragedies will exist," Bazel said. His dark eyes were half shut. "There's nothing we can do about them. But in the course of our work here at Chronos and our lives, every once in a while we can offer someone a future."

Shama thought that he sounded as if he should have trumpets behind his voice.

"It's a drop in the bucket of the universe of suffering but it's something," Bazel said. His confidence dropped off, and he spoke as if he were trying to convince himself.

Shama remembered her own disappointment when she found out she couldn't travel back in time to save her mother and what Bazel had said to her about his father: "Although we may not be able to save our loved ones, we can still save others."

After her race down the staircase holding onto Maye's purse, she understood what Bazel meant a little better now.

"How did you know?" Shama said.

"Know what?" Bazel said mildly.

Shama's head throbbed, and not from the blow but from the riddle of Maye. "About Maye and me."

Bazel nodded. "After the North Tower collapsed, I located Maye's purse."

Shama remembered Maye's clunky pink purse.

"And your bird's feather," Bazel was saying.

Her own BriZance, Shama thought tenderly. "Could you get me my bird back?"

Bazel shook his head and started to speak, but Pinkie interrupted, "Mungo's here." He disappeared back into the hallway.

"Your future is in your hands," Bazel said to Shama. "What's it going to be?"

While Bazel kept his gaze fixed on her, Shama pictured a feather lying in the rubble of a destroyed building. The feather of her bird. A puzzle piece from both the past and the future. And Maye Jones, Shama's great-great-grandmother, drawing a picture of her BriZance. Bazel had gotten Shama to attend the Academy so everything would be like it was meant to be from the beginning.

Pinkie returned to the doorway. "General Mungo, our patient has woken up," he called to someone in the hallway.

General Mungo stepped into the anteroom. His blue eyes looked genuinely concerned as he peered through the glass divider at the bed. "Lieutenant Bazel," he said. "Has she spoken yet?"

"No, General," Bazel said, his hooded lids lowering just a bit. "We were waiting for you."

As Shama closed her eyes and pretended sleep, she was glad to find wiggle room even in the puzzle of flade.

Acknowledgments

Thanks to Carolyn Coman, Justin Cronin, Tim Wynne Jones and Alex Parsons for your outstanding guidance and feedback, and to Brenda Liebling-Goldberg for your encouragement. A shout-out to Yellowstone Academy kids, Roneisha Gamble, Makayla Boles, Emerance Murekatete, Kristian Rockemore, Joneisha McFarland and Tiata Davis-Collier for reading the book. I'm grateful to my friend, Stephen Roxburgh, and namelos for holding down the lunatic fringe with excellence, integrity and faith. My godchildren Sara, Sonya, Mia and Nick, and special friends Iris, Tuck, Ryan, Dara and Katie—keep reading. My family—Bill, Elena, Will and Stephen—love you!

CPSIA information can be obtained at www.ICGtesting.com
260497BV00001B/2/P

9 781608 981069